"I'll come over tomorrow morning to babysit," she said.

Marc hadn't thought that far ahead. He didn't want to put her out or owe her. "No, that's okay. I've got it."

Her deadpan stare reminded him of his mother's. "You're in calving season. My brothers barely get more than three hours of sleep at a stretch when the cows are having their calves. You can't be everywhere at once. Let me take care of the twins—that way you can deal with the cows in the morning and then go to the hospital."

"Reagan…" He liked the way her name sounded when he said it. "I can't ask you to do that."

"You didn't ask. I offered." Her tranquility eased the chaos inside him. "Look, it's going to be weeks before my shop opens. I have time on my hands, and I love babies. I especially love these babies. These cuties melt my heart."

Her shop. Right. His mom's dreams. None of it seemed all that important right now.

What other options did he have, anyhow?

Jill Kemerer writes novels with love, humor and faith. Besides spoiling her minidachshund and keeping up with her busy kids, Jill reads stacks of books, lives for her morning coffee and gushes over fluffy animals. She resides in Ohio with her husband and two children. Jill loves connecting with readers, so please visit her website, jillkemerer.com, or contact her at PO Box 2802, Whitehouse, OH 43571.

Books by Jill Kemerer

Love Inspired

Wyoming Legacies

The Cowboy's Christmas Compromise
United by the Twins

Wyoming Ranchers

The Prodigal's Holiday Hope
A Cowboy to Rely On
Guarding His Secret
The Mistletoe Favor
Depending on the Cowboy
The Cowboy's Little Secret

Wyoming Sweethearts

Her Cowboy Till Christmas
The Cowboy's Secret
The Cowboy's Christmas Blessings
Hers for the Summer

Visit the Author Profile page at LoveInspired.com for more titles.

United by the Twins

Jill Kemerer

LOVE INSPIRED
INSPIRATIONAL ROMANCE

LOVE INSPIRED®
INSPIRATIONAL ROMANCE

ISBN-13: 978-1-335-59867-7

United by the Twins

Copyright © 2024 by Ripple Effect Press, LLC

For questions and comments about the quality of this book, please contact us at CustomerService@Harlequin.com.

Love Inspired
22 Adelaide St. West, 41st Floor
Toronto, Ontario M5H 4E3, Canada
www.LoveInspired.com

Printed in U.S.A.

Commit thy way unto the Lord;
trust also in him; and he shall bring it to pass.
—*Psalm* 37:5

To my Black Friday crew—
Eva, Ceci, Cali, Sarah, Olivia and Brandon.
You bring so much joy to my life. Thank you
for waiting with me in the BBW line for however
long it takes. I cherish our annual shenanigans!

Chapter One

After fifteen years, his mother's dream of expanding her bakery was about to come true. The stately brick building on the corner was finally available.

Marc Young inhaled the cold air, common for early April in Jewel River, Wyoming, and shoved his hands into his coat pockets as the door to Annie's Bakery clanged behind him. His mother, Anne Young, had opened the small shop when he was sixteen, not long after his dad had left them. If it hadn't been for her hard work and sacrifice, Marc wouldn't know where he and his sister, Brooke, would be today. He certainly wouldn't be the proud owner of the now-thriving ranch they'd almost lost.

His mom's patience was about to pay off. Over the years, she'd described her vision for the bakery countless times, always insisting the corner building was the only one that would do. Two months ago, Gus Prater had retired, leaving the former jewelry store empty.

It wouldn't be sitting empty much longer.

He turned toward his truck as a movement across the street caught his eye. A woman dug through a large purse on her raised knee near the corner building's entrance. The brick exterior boasted two huge picture windows to display Mom's donuts, cookies and freshly baked breads, and the ornate door had a transom window to let in light.

Marc couldn't place the woman. Her stylish outfit stuck out in their small town. Maybe she was the leasing agent Gus had mentioned when Marc had paid him a visit a few weeks ago about purchasing the building.

He'd been surprised to learn Gus didn't own the place. The man had kindly given him the contact information of the property manager, but she hadn't known much beyond the fact MDW Management held the deed. Marc's research showed that the late Dewey Winston had started the company, but no one seemed to know who'd taken it over after his wife's death last year. It was strange not knowing who made the decisions for the company.

Maybe this woman would have the answers he was looking for—mainly, how could his mother buy or lease the place? The last thing he wanted was for someone else to swoop in and steal it out from under her.

Marc looked both ways, then loped across Center Street, the main drag of downtown Jewel River. After a hop onto the sidewalk, he slowed his pace.

"Excuse me," he said as he approached the woman, still digging in that pit of a purse.

She straightened quickly, tossing a glance over her shoulder. Her face arrested him. Big light brown eyes—so light they were almost gold—widened under sculpted eyebrows. Her straight nose was sprinkled with pale freckles, and her lips were a raspberry tint he couldn't decide was natural or the result of gloss. Brown hair rippled down her back, and she was wearing a tailored dark gray wool winter coat with a cream-colored scarf carefully wound and tucked inside the neck. Slim-fitting black pants and tall boots completed the look.

Not from around here and dressed up? The leasing agent. She had to be.

"Hi there. I'm Marc. Marc Young." He circled to stand in front of her, forcing a welcoming smile as he nodded to her purse, still resting on her lifted knee. "Can I help you with that?"

She blew an errant lock of hair away from her face. "My purse? No, thanks. I've got it."

Her voice was melodic, smooth. As pretty as her delicate features.

"Are you here about the building?" he asked. He stretched his neck to peek inside the window closest to him, but without the lights on, there wasn't much to see.

"How did you know?" She lifted out a set of keys and hauled the purse straps onto her shoulder before giving him her full attention.

"Gus Prater mentioned you'd be coming by."

"Gus Prater?" She edged toward the door, gripping the keys. Was he making her uncomfortable? Didn't want her under the impression he was coming on too strong. He stepped back to give her more space. That should set her at ease. She hitched her chin. "The name isn't ringing a bell."

"Gus. The man who owned the jewelry shop for twenty years. This building."

"Oh, right." She stared at him and didn't move. Seemed to be waiting for him to continue on his way so she could unlock the door. Wasn't happening. This woman had no idea how important this building was to his mother. And why would she? They'd never met.

"My mom's been waiting years to open her bakery here." His palms were getting sweaty. What was his problem? He wasn't the nervous type. "So whether you're putting it up for sale or for lease, I want to be first in line. In fact, we could work out the terms now. Or anytime, really."

The woman gave her head a slight shake as her cheeks grew flushed. "I'm not putting it up for lease or selling it."

He rocked back on his heels. Then why was she there?

"You're not?" He tried to figure out what was going on but came up short. "You're the leasing agent, right?"

"No," she said quickly. "I'm Reagan Mayer. I own this building."

She *owned* the building? How was that possible? She seemed too young. He scrambled to regroup.

"Nice to meet you, Reagan," he said so quickly he might as well not have said it at all. "When you're ready to sell—or rent it out—give me or my mother a call. I can write down the contact information for you or text you my number if that's easier."

She tightened her hold on the purse and inched backward. "I don't think you understand."

"What?"

"I'm not selling or leasing this place. I'm starting my own business here."

Starting her own business? The words didn't

compute. Had she recently purchased it? How had she gotten the jump on him?

Why hadn't he known it was for sale?

"But you can't." He puffed out his chest as he firmed his stance.

"Why not?" Her head tilted in genuine curiosity.

"Because it's my mom's," he sputtered, kicking himself for being unable to form a cohesive argument.

"The deed's in my name."

"The deed is owned by MDW Management." He clenched his teeth, his molars grinding together. What was he missing? He felt blindsided and helpless and…upset. Really upset.

"I'm the sole owner of MDW Management."

"You?" He drew his eyebrows together. This woman—Reagan—couldn't be more than twenty-five years old. Twenty-six, tops. He gave her another glance. Okay, maybe twenty-seven. "How old are you?"

"Twenty-eight. Not that it's any of your business. How old are *you*?" Her offended tone alerted him he was crossing lines he shouldn't be crossing. *Get yourself under control. You've mastered the art of it over the years.*

"Thirty-two."

"What did you say you did again?" She narrowed her eyes.

"I own Young Ranch, about twenty minutes east of town. I'm also a member of Jewel River's planning and zoning commission. My mother, Anne Young, owns Annie's Bakery, across the street." He pivoted to point to the narrow building wedged between an insurance company and a dental office. Just seeing her tiny storefront gnawed at his heart.

His mom deserved this building. She'd risen before dawn for years and years to run the bakery, and she'd always clung to her dreams of expanding it right here, in the corner brick building.

This pretty outsider wasn't going to take it from her.

"What will it take to convince you to sell?" He crossed his arms over his chest. As soon as the words were out of his mouth, he knew they were the wrong ones to say.

"I'm not selling." Her lips drew into an offended line, and he expected to see sparks of fire in her eyes, but all he saw was resignation and a hint of vulnerability. "Now, if you'll excuse me."

He wanted to stand there and argue and convince her. But what would be the point?

He wouldn't let Mom's dreams be snuffed out. Not after all they'd been through. Not after all they were still going through. He'd find a way to get the building for her. He wasn't letting this get snatched away from her, too.

If only she wasn't such an unorganized mess, she would have easily found the key, unlocked the building and slipped inside before that unfortunate confrontation with Marc Young, the man she'd instantly dubbed Hot Cowboy.

Reagan Mayer waited until Marc was across the street before turning to unlock the door. She fumbled with the key, then unlocked it with a click, pushed open the gorgeous wooden door and went inside. She dead-bolted it behind her just in case anyone got ideas about coming in. And by anyone, she meant Hot Cowboy.

Her heart was still pounding over the encounter.

She'd taken one look at him and her mouth had gone as dry as the bread she'd popped into the toaster and forgotten about earlier. The man was tall—she guessed around six feet three inches—muscular and dressed like a typical rancher in jeans, cowboy boots, a Carhartt jacket and a simple Stetson on his head. His hooded brown eyes, straight nose, thin eyebrows and chiseled jaw all added up to gorgeous.

But then he'd gone and opened his mouth. She could handle a simple misunderstanding— clearly, he felt entitled to this building due to his mother—but his dismissive attitude? No. She couldn't handle that. And asking her age as if she were a twelve-year-old with no clue what she was doing? So condescending.

If only she'd had a snappy comeback. Her sister, Erica, would have had one; she always did. After getting divorced two years ago, Erica had moved to Jewel River to live with their great-aunt Martha on Winston Ranch. Then Martha had died, and Erica had inherited the ranch, while Reagan had inherited MDW Management, founded by her great-uncle Dewey. Her brothers had inherited Martha's investments. The company's assets comprised three commercial buildings, including this one, a hefty bank account and a small house four blocks away that had been sitting empty for more than a year.

With the help of her large family, Reagan had moved into the house on Saturday. Hard to believe she'd slept in it two nights already. It needed some TLC, but the two-bedroom home within walking distance to this beautiful building was perfect for her.

Let's see what I've got to work with. She inhaled deeply—it smelled dusty, old, with a hint of mildew—then flipped the light switches on. A sense of wonder filled her heart.

This was it.

Her chocolate shop would no longer be an idea she was chasing—it would be reality. Her reality.

Reagan brought her fists just under her chin, savoring the burst of delight rushing through her. She needed this. Needed a new creative venture. Needed to see if she could make it on her own away from her loving, and overbearing, family.

After spending her entire adult life working alongside her mother as they'd built a hugely successful online candle business—Mayer Canyon Candles—Reagan was ready to do things her way. And who knew? Maybe Jewel River would cough up the perfect guy for her in the process.

She wanted to get married and have her own family. But only with a man who accepted her and didn't try to change her mind when she decided to act on intuition rather than logic. Her parents affectionately called her a dreamer, and she supposed she was. An optimist, too.

The downside was that she'd spent her entire life avoiding conflict and ended up doing things everyone else's way. Not anymore.

Reagan set her purse on the counter and slowly ambled around the store, trailing her fingers along the dusty glass cases where the jewelry had been displayed. Then she studied the walls filled with shelves as she made her way to the back, where two offices, a bathroom, a break room and a storage space were located. A hallway led to the rear parking lot.

She returned to the main showroom and started picturing all of the chocolates she'd learned to make in Denver over the past six months as she'd apprenticed under a gourmet chocolatier.

Creating things—coming up with unique combinations—came naturally to her. It hadn't been much of an adjustment to switch from the precision required to make candles to the precision required to make chocolates. And now she could make her own special candies. Yes, a new creative challenge was exactly what she needed.

But first she had to get the business set up, along with all the paperwork, phone calls, permits and everything else necessary to remodel this building. It gave her a headache just thinking about it.

Maybe she *should* have asked Erica to join her today. Her sister was analytical and determined. She'd been the business end of Mayer Canyon Candles for several years. Plus, she used to run one of her ex-husband's dealerships and was in the process of creating an event center— the Winston—on her ranch. Erica was good at getting things done.

However, the whole point of Reagan coming to Jewel River was to make her own decisions. Find her own path. No more falling in with everyone else's ideas of what she should do and how she should do it.

Reagan rooted around in her purse until she found a notebook and pen. Then she leaned against one of the glass cases and began to sketch the space, leaving out the current displays and adding ones she'd need. As ideas came, she flipped to the next sheet to write them down inside random circles. She'd figure out how the ideas connected later.

Tapping the pen against her chin, she wondered how much of this she could keep. The maroon carpet was worn and faded. It had to go. A nice hardwood or vinyl-plank floor would work well in here.

She could picture the pretty navy boxes she'd picked out for the chocolates stacked on the shelves. Her sister-in-law Holly—a marketing genius—had been emailing her designs for logos. Reagan had narrowed it down to three, all with her company name: R. Mayer Chocolates.

Hugging herself tightly, she did a twirl. Then she stood still for a while to soak in the place.

She'd discussed her plan with her mom and two sisters-in-law. The three of them were now the heart of Mayer Canyon Candles. They'd all agreed Reagan's chocolates would be the perfect companion product to feature with the candles. They were adding a tab for R. Mayer Chocolates on the company's website to link directly to Reagan's online store once she was ready to open and had her website set up. This would allow her to sell the chocolates exclusively online until she had a feel for how much interest there was in them. Later, she'd bring on employees and open this store to the public.

A knock on one of the windows made her jump. *Please don't let it be Hot Cowboy.*

At the sight of Erica's face, Reagan let out a happy squeal and ran over to the door. She unlocked it and let her sister and Erica's three-year-old son, Rowan, inside.

"We thought we'd pop over and see how Auntie Reagan's doing, right, Rowan?" Erica waited for Rowan to hug her before coming in for her own embrace. "So, this is it, huh?"

Reagan nodded, her stomach starting to clench with nerves. This was where her outspoken sister would tell her exactly where everything should go and how she should do things. And if Reagan contradicted her, Erica would give her a skeptical look, the one she'd inherited from their mother. Then Reagan would second-guess herself and eventually do it Erica's way because *maybe* she was right. In her heart, though, she knew her way made more sense. Maybe not to anyone else, but it did to her.

"I love it! Look at these windows." Erica's eyes sparkled as she gravitated to one of the picture windows.

Reagan joined her. "It's going to be fun changing the displays seasonally."

"This place has so much character." Erica looked around in awe. Rowan was busy sprinting from one wall to the other in the open space behind them. "It's big. Way bigger than it appeared when the jewelry store was still in here."

Reagan slowly circled to take in the space. Now that Erica mentioned it, it *was* big.

Could it be too big?

Nah. Once she had the counters and sinks installed along the back wall, along with all the chocolate-making equipment and the racks, the space would feel just right.

"Slow down before you trip and fall," Erica called over her shoulder to Rowan.

"But I'm fast, Mama!" He continued running at top speed. "See?"

"I know you're fast. You'll probably run sprints in high school, but not in here." Erica turned back to her and rolled her eyes. "I can't wait for the weather to break. Keeping him cooped up indoors all day is wearing on my

nerves and Gemma's. She never complains,
though, unlike me."

"How is Gemma?" Erica's middle-aged house-
keeper/babysitter was a sweet woman. Very private, Gemma rarely left Winston Ranch.

"Great. Johnny Abbot finally got up the
nerve to come out and visit her last weekend.
I've never seen her so flustered. I told her they
could have tea in my house if she didn't want
him in her cabin, but shockingly, she declined. I
know she was nervous because she made three
kinds of cookies, apple bread *and* a sour cream
coffee cake."

"Who is Johnny again?" She couldn't remember if Erica had already mentioned him. Her
sister had shared so many stories about the various residents of Jewel River, and especially the
members of the Jewel River Legacy Club, that
Reagan had a hard time keeping them straight.

"The nicest man, Reag. He's sixty-five—
older than Gemma, but not by much—and he's
kind of shy but not as shy as she is. They went
to school together back in the day, and I think
he's got a crush on her."

"That is so sweet." Reagan loved the thought
of someday reconnecting with an old classmate
who had a crush on her. Except none of her old
classmates had ever had crushes on her, and her
dating life back home had been nonexistent. At

least in Denver she'd gone on dates with three men. They hadn't been the right guys for her, and that was okay.

The right guy was out there. Mom insisted he was. Of course, she also insisted that Reagan should settle down with a nice cowboy, and that hadn't happened. Still…a girl could hope.

Erica rubbed her hands together. "So, what's the plan with this place? What are you going to do first?"

Tempted to press the heels of her hands into her temples, Reagan forced herself to keep a cheerful demeanor. The looming tasks were daunting, yes, but she would figure it all out. Maybe.

"I'm not sure. Now that I'm here, I'll start getting a plan together."

"You'll need permits. Henry Zane is the building inspector. Nice guy. Oh, and did you file the paperwork to register the name of the chocolate shop yet? Once you get that done, you can get your Employer Identification Number and your online banking system figured out."

"Stop." She thrust her arms out. "I have plenty of time. I'm not going to rush. I haven't even unpacked my house, and this is the first time I've set foot in here."

"I'm not rushing." Erica flicked her fingernail against her thumb. "I'm simply excited for you. And I want to make sure every *i* is dotted and *t* is crossed."

"I know, and I appreciate your enthusiasm. But this isn't Mayer Canyon Candles. I'm older now. I'm capable of figuring it all out." At least, she hoped she was. One huge blessing from all of this was that she was financially secure. The buildings and bank account she'd inherited, along with her stake in the candle company, would pay her bills indefinitely. She could take her time learning how to get this business launched.

Erica gave her a look that screamed *if you say so* as she shrugged. "I'm glad you nixed the idea of using the other two buildings for your shop. They would not do at all."

She agreed with her sister there. One of the buildings was currently leased to a thriving convenience store, and the other, while empty, was more suitable for industrial work, not a retail shop.

"Well, if you can't get a hold of Henry—Angela's been keeping him busy—and you need help navigating the permits, call Marc Young. He's a member of the legacy club and on the planning commission. He can help you out."

Reagan was reasonably sure she grimaced at the sound of his name.

"What was that look for?" Erica asked.

"I met Marc. Right before I came inside."

"He's pretty cute, huh?" She waggled her eyebrows.

"Yeah." She left it at that.

"Uh-oh. What happened?"

"Nothing."

"Come on. I know you better than that."

She might as well give her the short version. Her sister would only pester her until she did anyhow.

"He seems to think his mom is opening a bakery here."

"Here? As in this building?" Erica cringed and peeked over at Rowan. He'd taken a toy car out of his pocket and was running it on the shelves as he made *vroom, vroom* sounds. "I didn't realize… I mean…it's well-known that Anne wants to expand her bakery. She's been waiting for the right space to open up. I didn't realize *this* was the space she had in mind."

"Do you think it's going to be a problem?" Reagan nibbled on her fingernail as visions of angry townsfolk boycotting her chocolates came to mind. She'd spent her entire life in a small town. She knew how they worked. Loyal to a fault, the residents would rally around Anne. Leaving Reagan—the newcomer—the loser.

"I hope not. She'll be disappointed, but she'll understand." Erica's gaze shifted toward the window. "But Marc? I don't know. He's like Jet. Protective of his mother and his sister, Brooke. And the past year has been awful for Brooke. Her husband died in an accident overseas— Ross was in the air force—and six months later she gave birth to identical twin daughters. That was back in January, so she has her hands full."

"Oh, no, that's terrible." Reagan's heart hurt for the poor woman. Losing her husband while pregnant? And having twin babies to raise on her own? "Does she live around here, too?"

"Yeah, Brooke moved back to Marc's ranch after Ross died. And once the twins arrived, Anne moved out there, too—temporarily—to help out with them. Anne has her own house here in town."

"It sounds like the entire family has their hands full." She bit the corner of her lower lip. "I feel bad about his mom and sister, I really do, but this building is mine. I said goodbye to everything I know—besides you—to move here."

"Exactly." Erica put her arm around Reagan's shoulders. "And once this town tastes your chocolates, all will be forgotten and forgiven, although there's nothing to forgive. Why don't you come to the legacy club meeting tomorrow night? You can meet the members. They'll love you. Have I told you how happy I am you moved here?"

"Only a thousand times. I'm glad I'm here, too." She hugged Erica again. Her big sister always had her back. "Now, enough about me. How is the pole barn renovation coming along? Will the Winston be ready in time for the wedding?"

"Oh, it will be ready." Her eyes got the scary fire in them that meant she was on a mission. Erica and Dalton's upcoming wedding reception would be the grand opening of the Winston. "Dalton has to be tired of my never-ending to-do list. But the pole barn—you wouldn't even recognize it. It's been transformed. There are special rooms for the bridal party, a stage for a band or DJ, a state-of-the-art sound system… You name it. I've got it."

"I can't wait to come out and see it."

"I can't, either. That reminds me—your maid-of-honor dress is a slightly different style than we originally planned. I'll show you later. If you hate it, we'll go a different route."

"I'll love it." She would, too, no matter what it looked like. She wanted Erica to be happy with a man she deserved, and Dalton was that guy.

After catching up for several more minutes, the three of them went back outside. Reagan blew Rowan kisses as he waved to her on the way to Erica's truck, and then she ducked her chin into her scarf and strode down the sidewalk toward her house.

She hoped Marc Young and his mother didn't cause problems. The chocolate shop was all she'd dreamed of for months, and Reagan wasn't settling for anything less. She'd done things other people's way her entire life. No one—not even a hot cowboy—could make her compromise this time.

Chapter Two

How could he get Reagan to see things his way?

The following afternoon, after a long day of calving, Marc was finishing up paperwork in his ranch office. His pregnant cows were having calves left and right, so he had to be on top of everything. Rico Hart, the full-time cowboy he'd hired a decade ago, was taking the night shift. The additional ranch hand Marc had hoped to hire for calving season had fallen through, and instead of putting out the word to find someone else, he'd opted not to hire anyone. He and Rico had made it through last year on their own. They'd get through this year, too. Marc just hoped the next couple of weeks didn't bring any major storms.

His life was stormy enough.

Yesterday he'd made a lousy impression with Reagan, and when he'd called around this morning to find out more about her, he'd been mortified to find out she was Erica Black's sister. He and Erica volunteered together for the Jewel River Legacy Club, and he didn't want there to be any bad blood between them. Because of her efforts, the members were motivated to improve the town.

Out of habit, he checked his phone, then let out a sigh of relief. No messages.

For months, his phone had been filled with texts from his mom. Marc didn't hold it against her. He was worried about Brooke, too. His little sister was four years younger than him, and he'd slid into the role of father figure after their dad deserted them. If Marc could wipe away the devastating events of the past year for her, he would in a heartbeat. Since he couldn't, he'd done the next best thing—moved her back home so he and his mother could help with his infant nieces, Megan and Alice.

Even with their help, Brooke wasn't bouncing back to her optimistic self, and Marc had no idea how to fix it. She'd lost all the baby weight and then some, and she'd barely gained enough during the pregnancy as it was. Dark circles had taken up permanent residence under her eyes, understandable with the twins.

The few times Marc had tried to help her with night feedings, she'd snapped at him. So he and his mother had formed a tag team during the day. As soon as Mom finished up at the bakery around noon—her part-timer closed shop at two—she rushed back to assist Brooke with the twins, and when Marc completed his ranch work by late afternoon, he helped with the babies while Mom made supper.

Again, he was struck by how much Brooke had been through—was still going through—and how much of a toll it had taken on his mother, too. It would be great to see Mom's face light up with the news she could finally expand her bakery. He hated letting her down.

Tracing his pen along the list on his legal pad, he reviewed his options. If he could just convince Reagan the building should go to his mom... But how? He didn't even know what she planned on doing with the place. A dozen potential stores came to mind, none of them good. A high-end clothing shop was the most likely option. Or maybe one of those smoothie bars so popular in cities these days. It could be a yoga studio or a tanning salon.

Yeah, you got all that in the two minutes you talked to her? Simply because she wore a dressy outfit? This is down-to-earth Erica's sister. The apple can't fall that far from the tree.

He thought back on how put-together Reagan had looked and how wary of him she'd been.

There was something different about her, and he couldn't put his finger on it. She made him feel off-kilter.

Maybe Henry Zane knew something about the building that he didn't. He reached for his phone. After the usual pleasantries, Marc got down to business. "There's a new owner of the old jewelry store. Know anything about it?"

"It's the first I've heard. Are you sure?" Henry asked. "Deed hasn't changed hands."

"I'm sure. Met her myself. She owns the company that holds the deed."

"You don't say." Papers shuffling and someone calling Henry's name were in the background. "I haven't heard a peep. Who is she?"

"Erica Black's sister."

"Huh. I assumed you were talking about an older gal."

"Not old. Young." Twenty-eight wasn't that young, though. His sister was the same age, and she was already a widow with twins. Again, he couldn't shake the feeling of helplessness pouring over him. Why did Brooke's life have to be so hard?

"Maybe Anne will finally get you married off." The man let out a throaty chuckle, which then turned into a coughing fit.

Marc ground his teeth together. He was *not* getting married. Weren't his hands full enough just running the ranch and making sure his sister, his mom and the twins were okay? And, at the moment, they clearly weren't.

"I don't think so," Marc said.

"She's ugly?" He sounded genuinely surprised.

"I didn't say that."

"Christy Moulten will likely have her eyes on the gal for Cade or Ty. She won't rest until those boys are married."

"More power to her." He personally didn't like the idea of either Cade or Ty Moulten dating Reagan. And he didn't care to think about why. "There isn't anything that would stand in the way of her opening a business here, is there?"

"None that I can think of offhand. Of course, it depends on what she's putting in there. You know as well as I do if she's renovating the building, she'll need contractors lined up before she can get her permit. Then there's state licensing."

For once, Marc wished he lived in a bigger town with stricter rules about local businesses. Then he could deny her the permit for whatever she was opening.

He winced. Since when had he become so mean and petty? He would never abuse his position on the planning and zoning commission to prevent someone from opening a business.

He was better than that.

A few minutes later, they ended the call, and this time when Marc checked, there was a text from his mother.

Can you pick up diaper cream before your meeting tonight? Alice has a rash and we're all out.

Without giving it another thought, he texted back that he would.

Closing his eyes briefly, he cleared his thoughts. *God, these women mean more to me than anything on earth. Whatever they need, please help me provide it. And pave a way for Mom to have her building.*

It was getting late. He'd better change so he'd have enough time to stop at the grocery store before the legacy club meeting.

A few minutes later, he strode down the path from the ranch office, located in one of the barns, to the farmhouse. He might not know much about Reagan and her plans, but tonight would be the ideal time to find answers. He'd simply ask Erica.

After he'd cleaned up and dressed in fresh jeans and a button-down shirt, he descended the staircase to the living room, where his sister was buckling one of the twins into a bouncy seat.

"I hear we have a rash situation?" He kept his tone bright, teasing.

"Alice is as cheerful as ever, but it looks painful." Brooke gave him a wan smile. He'd take it. It was better than nothing.

"And how is Miss Megan?" He bent over the play mat where Megan lay on her back, grabbing her feet. She was wearing a yellow sleeper with ducks all over it. He tickled her tummy, and she gave him a slobbery grin. His sister always dressed Megan in yellow and purple outfits, while Alice wore pink and pale green outfits. It made it easier to tell the girls apart.

"Happy as always. Nothing bothers her." Brooke looked as frail as a corpse as she knelt beside Megan.

"Why don't I get you one of Mom's sugar cookies and some chocolate milk?" He hated seeing her so pale and thin.

"And spoil my supper?" Her voice had an edge to it. "No, thanks. I'm fine."

Was she, though? She didn't look fine. She looked two steps away from the grave. He wasn't going to argue with her. It would only make her more defensive than she already was.

"Marc?" Mom called from the kitchen. "Can you come here a minute?"

He gave Brooke one last glance and made his way to the kitchen.

"What's up?" he asked, lifting the lid on the box of donuts she'd brought home. A cruller. *Yes.* He ate half in one bite.

She abandoned stirring the spaghetti sauce and turned to him as she wiped her hands on a towel. "The diaper cream."

"I know. You texted me." His mom assumed if she didn't remind him thirteen times, he'd forget.

"I took a picture of the tube for you."

"It's the same brand I bought two weeks ago, right?" He kept a lid on his temper. Mom was stressed out, too. This was her way of getting through it—by micromanaging everything.

"Yes, but I want to make sure it's the right one."

He stepped forward, putting his hands on her shoulders, and bent to kiss her forehead. "Don't worry, Ma. I'm taking care of it."

"Thank you." Her eyes gleamed with gratitude.

"You're welcome. Is there anything else I can pick up while I'm out?"

She craned her neck to peer through the archway that led to the living room. "She's too thin."

"I know."

"What if we buy that drink the nursing home uses?"

"I'll pick up some, but I doubt she'll touch it." Marc had been thinking along those lines, too. A nutritional drink might give her more energy.

"Grief is a terrible thing." Her eyes were

downcast. Then she returned to the stovetop and began stirring the sauce again. "I'll talk to her about keeping up her strength for the babies. Maybe a guilt trip will get her to eat more."

Yeah, like the guilt trips Mom had given him over the years had worked. They'd tended to annoy him. Although, to be fair, some of them had done their job.

"I've got to go."

"Don't forget—"

"The cream. I know."

"I'll text you that picture…"

As Marc went to the mudroom to put on his boots and coat, the feeling of not being up to the task overwhelmed him. It was the same feeling he'd had the first couple of years after Dad had cut himself out of their lives—incompetent.

He just didn't know what to do about his sister.

Sure, he'd invited Mom and Brooke to move back in with him so they could all work together to take care of the twins. He was glad they were here. It was a privilege to make sure his loved ones had what they needed. But no matter what he and his mom did, they couldn't get Brooke to eat more, and no matter how hard he tried, he hadn't made a dent in healing Brooke's broken heart.

Reagan's face came to mind with her faint

freckles and golden-brown eyes. Why did his thoughts keep returning to her? *Forget about her.* He was responsible for four women—his mother, Brooke, Megan and Alice. There was no room in his life for a fifth.

Now that she was here, Reagan was having second thoughts about attending the legacy club meeting. She wasn't the most outgoing person to begin with, and as soon as she'd entered the church's all-purpose room, she'd been swarmed. Apparently, the community center, where they normally held the meetings, was undergoing repairs and wouldn't be available until summer. Erica had promptly introduced her to a dozen people—Reagan had already forgotten most of their names—and the older ladies were peppering her with questions. They reminded her of her mother.

Christy Moulten, in particular, was overly interested in whether she had a boyfriend or not. Hopefully, the meeting would begin soon, and she could escape all this attention.

"Clem, this is my sister, Reagan Mayer." Erica appeared with a wiry, tough-looking rancher. At the sight of him, the ladies dispersed. "Reagan, this is Clem Buckley." His eyes were as hard as granite. A shiver tripped down Reagan's vertebrae. "He fills in for the building inspector occasionally. He can tell you what needs to be done."

Reagan *did* need help. She'd spent all day trying to determine the correct steps to start the business. The research she'd done online hadn't coughed up the information she needed. In fact, she'd gotten so bewildered by the various government sites with their food licenses, registrations and various permits she wasn't even sure she needed that she'd stretched out on the couch with a cool washcloth on her forehead for a good half hour.

She was never going to be able to figure out everything on her own.

"Building? What building?" Clem's voice was as hard as his eyes. Erica excused herself to organize her notes for the meeting.

"The brick one on the corner—" Reagan said.

"Jewelry store. Got it." Did the man ever blink? "What kind of business are you putting in there, girly?"

"A chocolate shop." She licked her lips. Maybe she should remind him her name was Reagan, not girly. Or maybe she should not speak at all so he'd leave her alone. The man looked to be in his seventies, and boy, was he intimidating.

He let out a *humph* and made a sucking sound with his teeth. "Who's going to buy enough chocolates to keep you in business in this little town?"

The town *was* small. It was just one of the reasons she'd decided to do the soft launch online before opening the store to the public.

"I'm selling them online at first."

"Then why do you need a big building?"

"I don't need a big building." She hated that her voice sounded so squeaky. "But I do need enough space for all the equipment to make them, as well as temperature-controlled display cases so I can select what I need for each box."

His skepticism was getting to her. Her breathing started growing shallow as all the reasons she never should have left the candle business came back in a rush.

"What about caramels?" He turned his head slightly and narrowed his eyes.

What about them? Did he have a problem with ooey-gooey deliciousness?

"I have my own recipe," she said. "I'm currently working on the perfect nut-and-caramel combo." She loved working with caramel. Making it from scratch required a lot of babysitting, and she'd learned the hard way not to stir it. But when it turned out right? Mmm... "Do you have something against caramels?"

"I do not." He straightened. "If there's a pecan or a peanut in there, I like 'em even better."

"You're really going to love my caramel collection, then." She went on to describe some of the chocolates she'd been mastering, and it was as if a weight was lifted from her shoulders. Discussing her craft always relaxed her. Clem asked more questions and his attitude softened. They were deep in a discussion about how much sea salt was too much sea salt when Erica asked everyone to find a seat.

Clem pointed to Reagan. "I'll talk to Henry Zane, the building inspector. He'll walk you through, nice and gentle-like, what you need to do to get the shop open." Then he patted her arm and—was that a smile?—retreated to the table.

Stunned, Reagan stood there a moment, then mentally shrugged before taking a seat next to Dalton Cambridge, Erica's fiancé. He leaned in and whispered, "We're in for a treat tonight. Angela Zane got her grandson to make a presentation for her Shakespeare-in-the-Park proposal."

"Jewel River has a theater club?"

"No, but that isn't stopping her."

"Is Angela related to Henry?"

"He's her husband."

Up front, Erica shushed them and they stopped talking. After the Pledge of Allegiance and the Lord's Prayer, the meeting got underway.

Reagan looked around the tables set up in a U and noted the people present. Christy had a good-looking cowboy next to her—no doubt one of the sons she'd mentioned—and Marc sat two spots down from him. Her heart did a funny skipping thing she didn't like. He was even more handsome tonight, and she hadn't thought it possible.

She wanted to resent Hot Cowboy for being overbearing and kind of rude yesterday when they'd met. But did she resent him? Not really. Couldn't fault the man for looking out for his mother. Her brothers would have done the same.

"I may have found a veterinarian." Cade Moulten, the handsome man next to Christy, was speaking. "As a bonus, her father is considering opening a training center for service dogs in the old warehouse on Birch Boulevard."

"That would kill two birds with one stone," Marc said. "We want those empty buildings filled."

"Does this woman have the know-how to treat large animals?" Clem, back to grumpy mode, was leaning back in his chair with his arms crossed over his chest.

"Yes," Cade said. "Although she primarily works with pets."

"We don't need our horses and cattle dying if the doc doesn't know which end is which," Clem said.

Cade gave him a pointed stare. "I can assure you she knows which end is which."

"I guess we'll have to take your word for it."

"I guess you will."

The meeting progressed, and Marc stood and gave an update on the empty buildings. One of them was the industrial building Reagan owned. She'd have to figure out what to do with it at some point. Another thing to add to her list. He glanced Reagan's way when he finished, and she didn't know how to interpret the look. It wasn't accusatory. If anything, it was questioning.

Clem rose, mentioned the progress on having a new sign made to welcome people to Jewel River, then waved his hand as if flinging off a bug. "I can't believe we're bothering to discuss this, but Angela, here, thinks having a Shakespeare-in-the-Park doohickey is a good idea. With that in mind, it's time to suffer through yet another production by her grandson. You've all been warned."

The lights dimmed, and everyone turned their attention to the screen. A couple dressed in medieval clothing held hands as they walked across a prairie. Suddenly, a computer-animated explosion filled the screen as hard rock instrumental music blasted through the speaker. The maiden or princess—Reagan had no clue—ran toward a fence as a bull charged in the distance. A man's deep voice rumbled, "Shakespeare like you've never seen it before. Wyoming style. Run, Juliet, run. Or the bull will take you down." Another explosion and fireworks completed the clip.

As soon as it was over, everyone looked at each other as if they weren't sure what they'd just witnessed. Reagan didn't know, either, but she couldn't help it—she started applauding. And everyone else joined in. Someone even yelled, "Bravo!"

Erica turned on the lights and resumed her position as the chair of the meeting.

"Thank you, Angela, for that lively presentation," Erica said. "And please tell Joey, good job. That boy has a future in Hollywood for sure."

"I keep telling him that, hon." Angela, a full-figured woman in her early sixties, beamed. "Just think what having Shakespeare here could do for the tourism!"

"Tourism? Bah." Clem shook his head.

For several minutes, the club members debated the pros and cons of hosting the event. Then Erica took control of the meeting and addressed Angela. "Why don't you put out a survey to find out how much interest there is for locals to participate in the play? We'd need actors, sets, costumes—all of it."

"Will do, hon." Angela nodded brightly, licked her finger and pretended to mark the air with it.

Across the table, Clem looked absolutely disgusted with life. His chin was tucked and his arms were still crossed over his chest. Erica moved on to the next topic.

After the meeting wrapped up, everyone stood to leave. Some of the women came back over to Reagan, including Christy, who appeared to be dragging her son with her.

"Reagan, I want you to meet Cade, my oldest son. His younger brother, Ty, was supposed to be here, but he must have gotten busy."

"Nice to meet you." She smiled up at him, and he grinned, thrusting his hand out.

"Good to meet you, too. I hear you're opening a chocolate shop in the old jewelry store."

"Yes, I am." He seemed pleasant enough. She gave him a self-deprecating smile and shrugged. "Well, I will eventually. Once I figure it all out." She spotted Clem out of the corner of her eye. "Clem is talking to the building inspector for me. Hopefully, he'll be able to guide me through the process."

"Clem?" Christy's eyebrows soared to her hairline. "Voluntarily?"

"Yes."

"He must have a sweet tooth," Cade said, still grinning. "I know I do."

"Or he was charmed by your sweet personality, Reagan." Christy gave her arm a squeeze. "I'm looking forward to spending *a lot* more time with you."

"Um, thank you." She didn't know what else to say. While Cade definitely seemed like a catch, Reagan had more important things on her mind. Like Hot Cowboy. She glanced at Marc again, but he was on his way out the door with everyone else.

Soon she joined Erica and Dalton, and they headed outside into the cold night air.

"Have you decided to paint any of the rooms?" Erica asked as they crossed the parking lot to their vehicles. "The house is so cute."

"I haven't made up my mind." She wanted to paint the living room, kitchen and her bedroom, but the right colors hadn't come to her. They would. They always did. She just had to give it time.

"When you know what you want, we'll come and help, right, Big D?" Erica elbowed Dalton's side.

"Of course. Just don't ask me to cut in the paint in the ceiling or corners. I'm all thumbs." He lifted his hands and wiggled his thumbs.

Reagan laughed. "I want to get things rolling with the shop first anyway."

They said their goodbyes, and Reagan noticed

Marc a few parking spots down. She hitched her chin to acknowledge him. He gave her a weak wave and got into his truck.

Disappointment sank to her belly. If she wasn't robbing his mother of her dream, maybe Marc would have been someone she could have gotten to know better. Or maybe not. Men were somewhat of a mystery to her.

If there was one thing Reagan knew, she wasn't getting involved with someone who would try to talk her out of something important to her. She'd already been there and done that with her parents, her siblings…and even herself.

It was time to stand strong. Even if her plans didn't make sense to anyone else. Especially if they didn't make sense to anyone else.

God had made her the way she was for a reason, and she was finally embracing it. Who cared if Hot Cowboy approved or not? This was her life, not his.

Chapter Three

He probably should have asked what this meeting was about. Almost a week later, on Monday, Marc opened the door to the building inspector's office in city hall. Henry had called him earlier to let him know he would be twenty minutes late to an appointment on his schedule. Since Marc always worked at city hall on Monday mornings for the planning and zoning commission, he'd assured Henry he'd handle the appointment until the man could get back. Marc was well versed on the typical questions people asked about permits.

He left the door open and took off his coat before sitting behind the desk.

"Hey, Marc, how are those babies doing?" Donna Marquez, one of the officers on duty, asked.

"The twins are great. Getting big. They sure are cute."

"And Brooke?" Her sympathetic expression only added to the guilt he couldn't shake off.

"As well as can be expected." He didn't know what else to say. It had been nine months since Ross had died. Brooke had loved him very much, and Marc wasn't sure if it was her grief, caring for infant twins—or both—weighing her down.

"Anything I can do to help?" Donna asked.

"Pray. Keep praying for her." As much as he was tempted to ask Donna for advice on how to get Brooke to eat more, he didn't. He'd picked up a six-pack of the nutritional drinks his mom had requested. Brooke hadn't touched them.

"You got it." She gave him a wave and continued down the hall.

Marc studied the desktop for a sticky note or any information clueing him in on what this meeting would be about. Someone looking to build a home? Maybe a problem with a commercial property?

He'd find out soon enough. And then he'd drive directly back to the ranch. Several cows would be having calves any minute now, and he needed to get out there to check on them. It wouldn't be long. A day or two, tops. He hadn't lost a calf yet this season. He planned to keep it that way.

A soft knock on the door had him looking up.

Reagan stood there, and as soon as she recognized him, she frowned.

"Oh, I'm sorry. I must have the wrong office." She stretched her neck back to check the plaque outside the door.

"Are you here for Henry?" Of all the meetings he'd been asked to fill in for, this was one he wished he hadn't agreed to.

He knew what this was about.

The building.

His mom's building. The one Reagan owned. The one she planned on keeping.

"Henry's running late. He asked me to fill in until he gets here." Marc gestured to the chair in front of the desk. "Have a seat."

He was proud of himself for sounding professional. He didn't want her to know how upset this situation was making him.

She slipped inside and closed the door. Then she unbuttoned her wool coat, revealing a lavender sweater, dark gray pants and dressy boots with a low heel. A delicate silver necklace with a cross hung at her collarbone.

"What can I help you with?" He folded his hands and set them on top of the desk, trying to keep his composure. Her hair had been pulled back in a low ponytail with loose tendrils escaping around each ear. Her long eyelashes made her eyes appear even bigger than he remembered.

"Um, maybe I should just wait for Mr. Zane."

His thoughts exactly.

"If you'd feel more comfortable, I understand." He gave her a tight smile.

She lifted her chin, and there was a hint of wariness in the gesture. Was she suspicious of him? Now he did feel like a jerk. He'd made a lot of assumptions when he'd met her last week, and they probably hadn't been fair.

"I take it you're here to discuss a building permit." There, he'd gotten the words out and hadn't sounded mad or upset. She nodded, her cheeks growing pink. "Where are you at in the process?"

She clutched her hands together. If there had been anything between them, it would be strangled to death by now.

"I was hoping to find out what the process is." Her honesty impressed him, but the words were still annoying. If she didn't even know the basics about how the permits worked, was she qualified to run a business?

"We have an application to fill out. You can download it online, or you can take one home with you." He swiveled the chair to grab a packet from the cubby behind him. Then he swiveled back and handed it to her. "It's in here, along with a list of contractors who are licensed to do the work. Call one of them—or all of them—and have them give you an estimate. They'll draw up plans, and then you can fill out the application and pay the fee. Once they start the work, there will be inspections."

"Okay." She was staring at the packet as if it were written in hieroglyphs. "Do I register my company's name here or the county or…?"

"Um, I believe it's with the state." Her question confused him, though. "I thought you owned MDW Management."

"I do, but I inherited it after my great-aunt died. My great-uncle was the one who started the company. Dewey Winston."

Ah…now he understood how she'd come to own the company. She'd inherited it. A blaze of annoyance crushed his forehead like a bad tension headache.

Inherited the company. From a wealthy relative. Who had those?

Don't be a hypocrite. Brooke had inherited a life-changing sum of money after Ross died. Her husband had been raised by his much older uncle. The late uncle's fortune had passed to Ross, which had then passed to Brooke upon his death. Because of the inheritance, his sister didn't have to work. She could be independent.

But Marc would have provided for her no matter what.

His heartbeat began pounding like a drum in the marching band. He wanted to ask Reagan if she had any idea how to run a business or if she was just doing this on a whim.

Chocolates. That was what he'd heard. She was opening a chocolate store.

Her knuckles were white against her clenched hands. "I never appreciated how much work my sister did for the candle company."

"Candles?" he asked. "I was told it was going to be a chocolate shop."

"Oh, it is." Her eyes shimmered as they grew wide. "My mother and I started a candle company about ten years ago. Erica joined us to handle the business side of things. I came up with the new scents, and Mom and I made every candle by hand. I loved it." Her face brightened as she spoke. "But I needed a change creatively and…well… I just needed a change."

A change. The freedom to quit a company, to move to another town? He'd never had the luxury. Never wanted it, either. He had no intention of doing anything differently with his life.

Reagan pushed her chair back. "I'll call the contractors you mentioned." She stared at the packet in her hand. "I want you to know that I didn't move here to ruin your mother's dreams.

When I realized the corner building was mine and that it was sitting empty, I felt like it was meant to be. I don't expect you to understand."

She had an honest, humble air about her, and her words drained some of the resentment he was clinging to. Before he could respond, his phone rang so loudly it made him jump.

His mom. She wouldn't be calling unless it was an emergency. The bottom dropped out of his stomach as he held up a finger to Reagan. "Give me one sec."

She nodded. He answered the phone.

"Marc, something's wrong with Brooke. She collapsed. I don't know if she fainted or what. I'm taking her to the clinic. Rico's here. He'll watch the babies until you can get back, but you've got to come home right away."

"I'm leaving now." He ended the call as his mind raced with fears. Brooke collapsed? He glanced at Reagan. "I have to go."

"Is something wrong? You look like you've had a shock."

"It's my sister. Mom's taking her to the clinic. I've got to get back for the twins. Rico is with them, but I don't know how good the cowboy is with babies." He realized he was babbling but was helpless to stop it.

Reagan stood, pointing to his coat hanging

on the back of the chair. He looked back, then snatched it and put it on.

"The twins are babies, right?" she asked.

"Almost three months old." He wiped his chin with his hand as his brain seized. He had to get home. Where were his keys? He tapped the pockets of his jeans, then his coat. There they were.

"Is your dad going with your mom?"

"What?" The question blindsided him. Dad? What was she talking about? "I don't have a dad. He left years ago."

"I'm sorry. I didn't know." She opened the door. "You should go to the clinic to be with your mom. I can take care of the twins."

"You?" He followed Reagan into the hallway.

"Yes. I've been taking care of babies for years. Your mom needs you. Your sister does, too."

Truer words had not been spoken. He'd just have to trust Reagan knew what she was doing. "Okay, do you want to follow me to the ranch?"

"Just text me the address. My phone will tell me where to go." She placed her hand on his arm. "I'll pray while I'm driving."

He clenched his jaw, nodded. Then they exchanged information, and he told her the basic directions to get to the ranch as they strode to the main door.

Reagan was right. His mom and sister needed

him. But he needed them, too. Needed them so much, it hurt to think about losing either one of them.

Reagan wanted babies. Her own babies. And holding these darling three-month-old twins, one in each of her arms, had kicked the urge into high gear.

"They're two little honeybuns, aren't they?" Rico, the middle-aged cowboy on baby duty, had a deep voice with a slight drawl. His brown eyes sparkled as he hovered nearby. He wasn't tall, but he was fit, with black hair that was graying at his temples. He'd set her at ease the instant she'd walked into the two-story farmhouse.

"That they are." She looked up at him and smiled.

"The boss has been awfully worried about their mama." The way he was tapping his fingers against his thighs made her think he was worried about her, too.

"Oh? Has she been having health problems?"

"I'm not sure. With her man dying and all…" His forehead wrinkled. "They'd only been married two years, and he'd been gone most of the one on active duty. Got killed in a helicopter crash somewhere in one of those oil countries."

At the thought of these babies potentially losing both parents, Reagan's eyes grew watery. She bowed her head. *Lord, these girls already lost their daddy. Please don't let them lose their mommy, too. Take care of Brooke, and comfort Marc and her mother.*

"I didn't mean to upset you." Rico held out a box of tissues to her. But her arms were full with the twins, so he set it next to her and took one of the girls.

"Thank you." She shifted the child and pulled out a tissue, dabbing her eyes with it. "I'm sorry. I'm just…"

"No need for sorries. I understand. Gets me right choked up thinking about it, too. Brooke had been living down in Texas before her man died. The boss moved her back into her old room after the funeral. No way he was letting her raise these honeybuns on her own. And then Miss Anne moved back in after they were born."

Hearing the tale from Rico gave her a deeper understanding of how difficult life must have been for Marc, his sister and his mother this year.

"I know it's not easy on her. Miss Anne likes being able to walk to work. It's harder for her now. Leaves here when it's still dark to get to the bakery, and then she helps out with the babies all afternoon."

It sounded exhausting.

"You don't happen to know how to tell the girls apart, do you?" Reagan studied the baby in her arms. The Cupid's bow lips, big dark blue eyes, long eyelashes and chubby cheeks absolutely melted her. Her plump little body nestled into Reagan's arms, and once more she was struck by how much she wanted one of her own.

"You're holding Megan, and I've got Alice."

"How can you tell?" With her finger, she caressed the girl's forehead along her hairline. Such soft skin.

"Brooke's got a system. Miss Anne told me that Alice is always in pink or green clothes, and Meggie's in light purple or yellow."

"Smart," she said. "I can take her back now if you'd like."

"Oh, I can stay a bit longer. It's not often I get to hold a wee one." He cradled the baby, and Alice stared up at him as if he was the most fascinating person in the world. The man was all cowboy, yet he looked perfectly comfortable as he made baby talk and cooing noises to the child.

"I don't get to hold them as often as I'd like, either." She was blessed with nieces and nephews, but now that she no longer lived in Sunrise

Bend, she didn't have daily access to them. "I grew up on a ranch with a big family."

"You missing them, huh?"

"Kind of. I mean, my sister—Erica Black, you might know her—lives nearby. The twenty-minute drive from my house to her ranch is nothing. But the rest of them? Yeah, I'm not used to being on my own."

"Well, when you're feeling lonely, remember the Good Lord is always with you. My mama told me those words just about every day of my life. She still does. She's in the nursing home in town. It's small, but it gets the job done."

"I didn't realize there was a nursing home here. That's wonderful."

"It sure is. I couldn't take care of her anymore after she broke her hip. Now I can visit her every day and not worry about her falling."

Little Megan stretched her arms up and arched her back as her face scrunched and grew red. "Uh-oh. I think she's either getting hungry or going to need a change soon."

"Miss Anne left bottles in the fridge. She said they'd be hungry about this time. Why don't I warm 'em up?" He brought Alice to the infant seat on the floor and set her in it. She instantly began to whimper.

Reagan stood and settled Megan in the one next to Alice's. Then she knelt in front of them and talked to them as she made funny faces while Rico got the bottles ready. Neither baby was impressed with her attempts to entertain them. They both looked on the verge of tears.

Did they have pacifiers? She looked around, but all she could find were plush baby toys and a few receiving blankets.

"Here you go." Beaming, he brought two bottles over. "I checked 'em and everything."

"Thank you." What a nice man. She squirted a drop onto her wrist—not too warm, not too cold. "These are perfect."

She gave one to each baby and held the bottles as they greedily reached for them.

"I hate to leave you, but the boss will have a fit if one of our pregnant cows has a calf and I'm not out there monitoring the situation."

"I understand. Thank you for all your help."

"Let me give you my number if you need anything. I can be back lickety-split." He wrote down his cell number and left.

The babies had settled down after the initial gulps, and Reagan studied them as their eyelids began to droop. They truly were identical. She couldn't see anything different between them.

Brooke's situation reminded her of her late brother, Cody. Years ago, when he died in a car accident, his wife, Holly, had been pregnant with their child. No one in Reagan's family had even known Cody was married, let alone having a baby, though. And, weirder still, Holly was now married to Reagan's big brother, Jet.

Cody. Reagan sighed. He'd been the sibling closest to her in age. The baby of the family. A wild one. And being estranged from him the months before his death would hurt until the day she died.

She'd done the right thing coming here today so that Marc could go to the clinic to be with his mother. Hopefully, it wasn't anything serious. But if it was...

What her own parents would have done to be with Cody one more time before he died. What *she* would have given to see Cody one more time and tell him all the things she'd desperately wanted to say.

Someday she would. That was why she clung so tightly to her faith. She knew this world wasn't where it ended. In the meantime, she'd make the best of her time here, and feeding these babies was at the very top of her list.

Marc dragged himself to the house later that evening. This morning felt like a lifetime ago.

Reagan's white crossover SUV was still parked next to Brooke's minivan. Would his sister ever drive it again? There were so many unanswered questions about her health.

He trudged up the steps to the side door and quietly let himself inside. In the mudroom, he took off his coat and boots and just stood there for a few moments.

Come on. You're used to this. Gird your shoulders. Get your game face on. You need to be strong. Reagan helped you out today. After she leaves...well, then you can fall apart.

That was the thing, though. He couldn't fall apart. Ever.

Too many people depended on him.

Falling apart would only result in him failing them. And he wasn't about to go down that road.

He straightened his shoulders and strode through the mudroom and kitchen. Continued to the archway into the living room and stopped in his tracks.

Reagan was rocking in the recliner with a baby in each arm. She was telling them a story—but no book was in sight. He leaned against the archway and listened as she went on about a girl with flowers for hair fighting a giant who was trying to cut down the tree she lived in. His lips twitched. Couldn't help it. Reagan was an original.

She looked up and their eyes met. Hers were so expressive. Surprise turned to welcome glimmering with sympathy.

"How is she?" she asked. The melodic tone of her voice soothed him.

He shoved away from the archway and padded to the couch, where he took a seat and let his head fall back against the cushion.

"Not good. She had a stroke."

"Oh, no!" Reagan kept her voice low as she glanced at the twins, almost asleep. "She's going to make it, though, right?"

Her concern surprised him. She'd never met his sister. Had no reason to care. Yet she did.

"It appears that way. Mom said the clinic thought it was a migraine at first, but they grew concerned when they examined her, so they rushed her to the hospital in an ambulance. Her left side is weak, but not paralyzed."

"A stroke." With her forehead furrowed, she shook her head. "But she's young, right? How old is she?"

"Twenty-eight." He swallowed as everything hit him at once. His little sister could have died today. She still wasn't in the clear. And what if she didn't get full range of movement back in her left side? How would she be able to take care of the twins?

He should have insisted she eat more. She hadn't been taking care of herself. Over the past weeks, she'd been vanishing before his eyes. He should have tried harder...

"Do they know what caused it?"

He inhaled sharply through his nose. "They're running tests. Her risk increased because of her history with migraines, and it was also elevated due to having the babies, although postpartum strokes are rare." He didn't even know what he was saying at this point. Just repeating things the doctors had said. He raked his fingers through his hair. "Never in a million years would I have thought my sister could have a stroke at her age."

"How is your mom holding up?"

"Good." It was true. His mom had been calm. Asked all the right questions. "She refused to leave her side. She's staying there tonight."

"My mom would have done the same. My dad, too." Her sympathetic expression was like the hug he needed, and all he wanted to do was to go over there and have her put her arms around him and tell him everything was going to be all right.

He must be losing it. Wanting a virtual stranger to comfort him? Unheard of. Uncalled for. He was the one who comforted, not the other way around.

"Do they have any idea how long she'll be in the hospital? By the way, what hospital did she go to?"

"She's at the medical center in Casper."

Reagan stared down at the babies, both now asleep on her lap. Her face was full of love for the girls, and gratitude filled him that the twins had been in good hands. One thing he hadn't had to worry about, anyway.

"I'll come over tomorrow morning to baby-sit," she said matter-of-factly.

He hadn't thought that far ahead. He didn't want to put her out or owe her anything. "No, that's okay. I've got it."

Her deadpan stare reminded him of his mother's. "You're in calving season. My brothers barely get more than three hours of sleep at a stretch when the cows are having their calves. You can't be everywhere at once. Let me take care of the twins. That way you can deal with the cows in the morning and then go to the hospital. Your mom will need the moral support."

"Reagan…" He liked the way her name sounded when he said it. "I can't ask you to do that."

"You didn't ask. I offered." Her tranquility eased the chaos inside him. "Look, it's going to be weeks before my shop opens. I have time on my hands, and I love babies. I especially love these babies. These cuties melt my heart."

Her shop. Right. His mom's dreams.

None of it seemed all that important right now. What other options did he have, anyhow?

The bakery would be short-staffed. Hopefully, Mom had called her employee, Deb, about getting someone to help her out tomorrow. All the pregnant cows he'd been keeping an eye on needed to be monitored. Rico had texted him that only one had given birth.

"You're overthinking it." Reagan's voice cut through his thoughts. "I'll be here at seven."

"Okay." He felt out of his league. "I'll show you where everything is and go over their schedule in the morning."

"Don't worry about this, Marc. I'm good with babies. You worry about the other stuff. Leave these two sweethearts to me."

A sigh escaped his lips. Reagan was right. He had enough other stuff to think about. Not having to worry about the babies would be a huge relief. Not just for him but for his mom, too. And Brooke, when she gained full consciousness. She'd still been out of it when he'd left.

"I don't know when my sister will be discharged. I'll have to find someone to help me out with the twins until then."

"No, you won't." She smiled, shaking her head. "I'll babysit them while your sister is in the hospital."

Marc couldn't help admiring her. "Thank you. I don't know what to say but thank you."

"You don't have to say a thing. Now, let's get these babies to bed so you can get some rest."

He wouldn't argue with that. It had been the longest day of his life, and something told him the rest of the week would be just as rough. He was grateful for Reagan's help. And he would find a way to repay her when all this was over. He just had no idea how.

Chapter Four

Reagan was used to detours in her plans. She rarely fretted over schedules or deadlines. Even when the unexpected happened—like twin babies needing an emergency babysitter—she trusted God would give her the time and tools she needed to meet her goals. The few times she hadn't met them? It wasn't for lack of trying. So, this detour in her plans didn't bother her one bit. The only thing that bothered her was the fact it was for Marc.

At six forty-five the next morning, Reagan parked next to the minivan in his driveway and took a moment to mentally prepare herself. She'd brought her laptop, a notebook and the packet Marc had given her yesterday morning. Would she have a chance to research anything? Maybe. Maybe not. At least she had what she needed if she got any downtime.

Last night she'd called her mom and talked for an hour about the twins and Brooke, how the candle shop was doing and all the latest from Sunrise Bend. Reagan missed her mom. They'd worked well as a team, and she'd learned everything about taking care of babies from her, too. So far, the twins seemed to be easygoing. She hoped it stayed that way.

She closed her eyes and said a quick prayer for Brooke. Then she took her large tote and purse in one hand, grabbed her travel mug of coffee with the other and stepped out onto the gravel. She shut the door behind her. The cold air was bracing against her face. The peach-and-periwinkle sky against the rising sun tempted her to take a picture, but her phone's camera would never do it justice.

As she walked toward the porch, she took in the ranch and couldn't help comparing it to the one she'd grown up on. Marc's was smaller in scale. No guest cabins, fewer outbuildings. In the distance, cattle roamed the pasture. The ranch might be smaller than her family's, but it was well-kept. Marc seemed like the type of man who cared about the details.

She reached the porch and knocked on the door. The door opened and Marc, bleary-eyed and unshaven, appeared. His button-down shirt was untucked, and he held one of the twins in the crook of his arm. The other twin was crying from somewhere inside. Probably the living room. "Oh, good. You're here. Come in."

He held the door open until she'd cleared the doorway, then shut it behind her and stalked to the living room. She followed. Yep, there was a baby in purple—Megan—kicking her legs and bunching her fists as she wailed from her bouncy seat.

Reagan set the travel mug on the end table and dropped her bags to the floor before unbuckling the child. Then she lifted her up to her shoulder, bouncing slightly as she made shushing sounds. "It's okay, Meggie. I know you miss your mama. It's okay."

"How did you know it was Megan?"

She turned to Marc. "Rico told me the secret about their colors. She wears yellow and purple. Alice wears green and pink."

The baby's cries were intense. Reagan figured it would take some time for her to calm down. However, a few moments of bouncing and cooing soothing words downgraded the wailing to whimpers. With a sigh, the child rested her cheek on Reagan's shoulder. Reagan rubbed her back, basking in her surrender.

"I don't know how you got her to stop crying." The bags under Marc's eyes and his general air of defeat brought a wave of sympathy over her.

"Are they hungry?" she asked.

"No. I fed them both before you arrived. And they had bottles at three."

She winced. It had to have been exhausting getting up with the babies after the day he'd had yesterday.

"Diaper change?" she asked.

"Fresh. Ten minutes ago."

"Maybe she's gassy." Reagan kissed the top of Megan's head and continued to caress her back. "Or she just misses her mama."

"I don't know." From the pinched expression on his face, she guessed the crying had given him a headache.

"Did you try a pacifier?"

"They never took to them. Spit them out from day one." Alice looked content as could be in her uncle's arms. He stared longingly at the couch, but he didn't sit.

"Ah. Does Brooke have a routine with them?"

"Yes. Rule number one—they do everything together. They eat at the same time. They nap at the same time. Brooke said she'd get zero hours of sleep if she didn't keep them on the exact same schedule. I don't really know what the schedule is beyond what I help with. Usually, I get ready, come down and change them out of their pajamas into clothes while Brooke grabs a shower. As soon as she's dressed, I head out."

Reagan tried to wrap her mind around the fact Hot Cowboy dressed two babies every morning. "Any word on how your sister's doing?"

"I talked to Mom earlier. She's the same."

That wasn't good. She'd hoped he'd have some indication his sister was recovering.

"Are you going over there today?"

"Yeah, as soon as I finish checking the pregnant cows and talking to Rico."

"Why don't you bring your mother a fresh change of clothes and some toiletries? I'm sure she'll appreciate it."

"I didn't even think of that." He brightened. "I will."

"I won't keep you. I've got this. You can take off."

"Are you sure?" He tried to tuck in his shirt one-handed.

"Of course."

"What if she starts crying again?" The way his eyes narrowed reminded her of her family's skepticism whenever they thought she was in over her head.

"We'll be okay." She shrugged. "I have a good feeling about it."

"A good feeling? About this? I'm glad someone does." He rubbed his chin. "Let me show you where we keep everything."

"I can figure it out. I found what I needed yesterday."

"It will only take a minute."

They proceeded to go upstairs. Reagan still held Megan and Marc carried Alice. He showed her where the twins slept in the bedroom next to their mother's. He pointed out diapers, lotions, clothes and blankets before returning to the hall and pointing to the right. "My mom's here. I'm down at the other end."

Reagan clutched the baby as she followed him down the staircase and into the kitchen, where he showed her the formula, bottles, bibs and everything else she might need. She'd found most of it yesterday, but it was still good to take the tour.

"Thanks." She craved her coffee. "If I need something, I'll text you."

"Okay." His jaw flexed twice. Then he brushed past her to return to the living room. She joined him as he crouched to buckle Alice into her bouncy seat. Then he tapped the tip of his finger on her little nose and told her to be good today before he straightened. Turning to Reagan, he kissed the top of Megan's head, and the scent of citrus and leather wafted to her. Whatever cologne or bodywash he used was as appealing to her as the affection he freely gave to the girls. Very appealing indeed.

"Thanks again." He gave Reagan a lingering look she didn't know what to make of and then strode out of the room. A few minutes later, the creak of the side door reached her, letting her know she was alone with the twins.

"Well, my darlings, it's just you and me now." Dare she attempt to set Megan back in the seat? Her gaze landed on the travel mug. Her coffee was calling her name. "Miss Meg, how do you feel about hanging out with your sister? I'll squish your seats together so close you two can hold hands if you want. Would you like that?"

Reagan bent to put Megan in the bouncy seat, and the baby's little lips began to wobble. "It's okay, sweetie. I'm right here. I'll be here all day."

As the wobble grew more pronounced, she buckled the straps and began to hum. The babies seemed to like it, so she hummed louder while she retrieved her coffee, still hot, along with her tote bag and purse. Maybe the girls liked music.

She found her phone and swiped through a radio app until she found a nursery-rhyme songs playlist. Soon, both the girls were happily kicking their little legs and reaching for the toys dangling from the toy bars.

They were so precious. She couldn't help herself—she took pictures of them both. Maybe Marc could send them to his sister. It would help Brooke not to worry about the babies. She'd know they were in good hands.

Good hands? Reagan didn't consider herself a baby expert by any means, but she'd learned a thing or two over the years from her mother and from babysitting her nieces and nephews. The most important thing was not to panic. Babies got fussy; they cried; they gulped down their bottles one day and barely touched them the next. And teething was no fun. No fun at all.

"You two aren't ready to get your teeth yet, are you?" She hoped they weren't. Megan blew a spit bubble. "I'll take that as a no."

As she drank her coffee, she decided to take advantage of this sliver of quiet time to get out her notebook. She looked over everything, but the big picture of what needed to be done still wasn't coming to her in a meaningful way. After digging around in her purse, she found a pen and drew a circle in the middle of a fresh sheet of paper. In it, she wrote Store Opening.

Then she created more circles and wrote tasks in them—Contractors, Estimates, Banking, Renovations, Licenses. As more tasks came to her, she gave them circles, too. Then she studied the paper and drew lines between any that related to each other.

Okay, it was starting to make sense. Sort of.

Alice let out a chirp, and Megan began pumping her legs. The twins were getting restless. Time to get them out of those seats. She set her notes aside and unstrapped one baby, picked her up, then unstrapped the other and awkwardly picked her up, too.

How did Brooke do this all the time? Not only was trying to carry two squirmy babies difficult, but it strained her muscles. Her arms and back were still sore from babysitting yesterday.

Maybe she needed to start lifting weights. *Yeah, right.* As if that was going to happen. She wasn't much of an exerciser. She let out a snort. That was an understatement.

Reagan took the twins to the couch and carefully sat down, then adjusted them on her lap. Alice yawned and snuggled deeper into her arms, while Megan curled her hand around Reagan's pinkie finger and stared up at her.

"You're not so sure about me, are you?" Reagan smiled at Megan. *"Who is this weird lady and what did she do with my mommy?* Well, pumpkin, I'm just filling in. Your mommy will be back soon."

She hoped it was true. It reminded her once again that life was short. She had no idea how much time on earth she had, and she needed to make the most of it. All she had to do was think of Cody to know it was true.

Once the girls fell asleep, she was going to

take out her laptop and figure out what she needed to do to get her business name registered. Marc had said to take care of it with the state, right? Until then, she'd enjoy the babies.

"Why don't I tell you a little story? It's about a girl named Reagan, who wanted to open a chocolate shop. She learned all about how to make the chocolates from a kind man named Oliver, who owned a fancy store in faraway Denver. Every time she got a whiff of the rich scent of chocolate, she could picture the pretty candies lined up in their boxes. But Reagan had a problem. Before she could open her shop, she had to fight a scary beast called the Paperwork Monster. The Paperwork Monster was big and mean, and he told her if she didn't have all of her forms completed just right, she wouldn't be able to make the chocolates…"

Megan was wide-awake, drooling all over her tiny fist, which she'd somehow managed to fit in her mouth, and Alice was smacking her lips occasionally as she listened. These two darlings made all Reagan's problems seem like she could make them disappear with a poof.

Her problems were tiny compared to Marc's. Up in the night feeding the girls, doing the morning routine alone, riding out to check the cattle, driving to the hospital to be with his mother… He was destined to crash if Brooke stayed in the hospital for several days.

He seemed the type of guy who didn't ask for help often. But he needed it.

Reagan shifted on the couch to get more comfortable. The twins were growing sleepy, and she'd wait a bit to put them in their Pack 'n Plays, where Marc said they napped. Once they were asleep, she'd prepare more bottles and get some work done…if she had time.

Something told her she wouldn't be getting much research done today. Erica and her mother would insist she needed to stay focused. But the only focus she cared about at the moment was on the twins. Getting the rest of her life back to normal could wait.

Life wasn't going to be returning to normal anytime soon.

It was after eight that evening when Marc arrived home from the hospital. He hung up his coat and washed his hands in the mudroom before dragging himself into the kitchen. Reagan was sitting at the table and typing away on a laptop. She looked up at him and smiled.

"How did it go?" she asked.

Closing his eyes momentarily, he traced the arcs of his eyebrows, trying to alleviate the pressure in his head. "Not good."

Reagan went to the oven and pulled out a covered casserole dish. "I kept it warm for you. I wasn't sure if you and your mom had eaten."

"You cooked?" He couldn't believe it. She'd spent over twelve hours here babysitting the twins and had somehow found time to make supper? He'd underestimated her, and it only added another layer of guilt to his already full load.

"Yeah, it was tricky, but I did it in shifts. Chicken-and-stuffing casserole—it comes together quick. If you've already eaten, I understand."

"I didn't. We didn't." He removed a plate from a cupboard and dished out a large helping of the casserole. It smelled good. "Thank you. For this. For the girls. For…everything."

"You're welcome." She returned to the table, sat down and closed her laptop.

He took a seat across from her and dug in. It was delicious. Comfort food—exactly what he needed. He ate several bites before setting aside his fork. He needed to update Reagan on Brooke. But putting it into words? He dreaded it. Saying it out loud would make it all real. Too real.

He wished reality would go away. Wished Brooke was there. Wished Mom was, too.

"Why don't you finish your food before you tell

me everything?" Her light brown eyes brimmed with sympathy, and her patience astounded him.

He wasn't all that patient. Brooke wasn't, either. Mom had the most patience of the three, but even she had a limited supply. Reagan seemed to have it in abundance.

"Okay." Agreeing with her was simple, a relief. If he wasn't so exhausted, he'd force himself to be strong and tell her everything now. To get it over with. But he didn't have to. She'd given him permission to eat his meal, and the simple gesture meant everything to him at the moment.

He almost made it through. Almost finished chewing the final bite. But all of his emotions hit him at once. He tried to swallow but couldn't. So, he spread his palms out on the table with his head bowed, willing himself not to choke, or worse, cry. Somehow, he forced down the final bite of food. Then he blinked and tightened his jaw.

"Do you want a glass of water?" She stood and tucked the laptop and her notebook into a large bag on the floor next to her chair.

"No, that's okay." That seemed to do it. A sense of calm chased away the intensity of his emotions.

"If it's too much to talk about, we don't have to—"

"No, I'm ready." He hoped he was, at least.

Watching him expectantly, Reagan returned to her seat.

He pushed the empty plate to the side and took a moment to get his thoughts straight. "We know more now. She had an ischemic stroke. Due to Mom's quick thinking and the clinic immediately sending Brooke to the hospital, the doctors were able to give her a special medicine to dissolve the blood clot that was preventing blood from getting to her brain. It's supposed to help her recover more fully than if she didn't have it."

"That's good news."

"Yes, it is." He just wished the rest of the news was good. "Unfortunately, she's really weak. She's in and out of it. Doesn't really know what's going on. Can't speak very well. We only understood a few words. Her left side has limited strength. She isn't paralyzed, but she'll need physical and occupational therapy."

"Will she recover?"

"Most likely." But what if she didn't? He wouldn't think about that now. "The doctors estimate she'll be in the hospital for a week."

"Then she'll come home?" Her hopeful expression hurt his heart. It matched the hope he'd been clinging to before the doctors had filled them in.

"Doubtful. Unless she shows outstanding

progress over the next few days. They think she'll be transferred to a rehab facility." His throat was thick with emotion. He couldn't say another word if he tried.

"Can she eat and drink?"

He nodded, grinding his teeth together so hard, he was shocked none of them chipped.

Reagan got out of her chair and rounded the table to him. Then she wrapped her arms around his neck and leaned in to hug him.

"I'm so sorry, Marc."

Tears threatened. Reagan gently rubbed his upper back as she held him, and slowly, the out-of-control feelings passed, and he allowed himself to relax into her embrace.

He needed her gentle touch. Needed her comfort.

She pulled away, went to the cupboard next to the sink and grabbed a glass, then filled it with water and brought it back over to him. His fingers grazed hers as he took it from her. "Thanks."

He wished she'd hold him again, but she was already sitting down. He took a long drink of the water.

"Can I pray for you and your family?" Reagan asked.

"Right now?" he sputtered. He went to church. Prayed before meals and when things were rough. But his family had never been demonstrative in the prayer department. Her shy nod helped push away his qualms. "Sure."

"Lord, You are all-powerful and know what Brooke needs. Please heal her from the effects of the stroke. Give the doctors and nurses and everyone taking care of her wisdom and skill as they treat her. Please comfort Marc and his mother as they adjust to this terrible turn of events. Help them trust You and rely on You as she recovers. In Jesus's name, amen."

"Amen." Her prayer touched him, but it also brought up uncomfortable feelings and questions he wasn't sure what to do with.

This terrible turn of events... Why had God allowed this to happen? Hadn't Brooke been through enough this year? And Reagan assumed Brooke would heal, but what if she didn't? What if she ended up unable to speak or to get dressed or to walk or to take care of Megan and Alice?

But the biggest question was the one he'd been flirting with for years and years. He'd never let himself sit with it long enough to get a satisfying answer.

Could he trust God?

Marc shifted his jaw and glanced up at Reagan. She seemed embarrassed.

"I don't normally go around praying for people like that," she said with her head hung low.

"I don't, either. But I appreciate it."

"The moment just seemed to call for it."

That it had. "I haven't had time to figure out a plan for the girls."

"Plan? No need." Her steady gaze implied everything was already worked out. "Until we know more, I'll keep coming over at seven, and I'll call my sister about getting some of the church ladies to take over in the afternoons. They'll be chomping at the bit to spend time with the twins. They'll probably bring food with them, too, so supper will be taken care of. You'll still have to get up with the girls at night, though. When do you think your mom will be coming back?"

Church ladies? Reagan here every morning? His house was going to be invaded. It was too much to take in. He gulped.

"Mom booked a room at a hotel near the hospital. Thankfully, she has her car, too. Her employee, Deb, asked her cousin to help out at the bakery in the mornings until she gets back. By the way, Mom appreciated the clothes and stuff I packed her. Thank you. I wouldn't have thought of that on my own."

"I'm glad. You were smart to pack more than one outfit." Reagan lifted her finger. "Oh, I forgot. I took pictures of the girls today. I'll text them to you to send to your mom. I'm sure

Brooke will need some reassurance that the babies are doing all right."

Her fingers flew over the phone and, moments later, his chimed. He opened her text and instinctively smiled. The twins were clearly happy with Reagan.

"You don't have to do all this, you know." He leaned back, massaging one shoulder. "I can find someone else to help with the twins."

"Like I said, I want to. I have the time. It will be a while before I can open the shop."

The shop. He winced. He kept forgetting she owned the building of his mother's dreams. At this point, it was the least of his worries. The only thing he really cared about was getting Brooke back here. Healthy. Healed.

He didn't know how this stranger had popped into his life and solved so many problems at a critical time, but…well, that wasn't true. Reagan's prayer had shifted something inside him. He could clearly see God's hand in her being there.

Maybe he *could* trust God after all.

He couldn't get attached to her, though. He already struggled to be the man his sister, his nieces and his mother needed.

But he could still feel her gentle hands as they'd rubbed his back, and he wondered if he was wrong. Was there enough of him to go around to get close to Reagan, too?

No, there wasn't. A couple of days and he'd be himself again. He'd make sure of it.

"I feel terrible for them." Reagan stretched her arms over her head and savored the sensation of her tight muscles starting to loosen. She had her earbuds in as she talked to Erica on the phone. She'd gotten home from Marc's ranch an hour ago.

The day had been long. Fulfilling, but long. Those little babies had worn her out.

"They don't have any idea if Brooke will recover?" Erica asked. "You know, fully?"

"Not right now they don't. I hope over the next few days she'll get better and better so she can skip the rehab facility." Reagan swung her legs up on the couch, then leaned back against a throw pillow and wiggled her toes. Her fuzzy pink slipper socks felt soft against her skin.

"I hope so, too, but even if she did…well, I think she'll need help for a while."

"Yeah, I think you're right." Reagan reached for her mug of hot tea and took a sip. Perfect. Not too hot. Not too cold. Just right.

They discussed inviting the church ladies to help with the twins.

"I tell you what," Erica said. "I'll call Christy

and explain the situation tomorrow. That way you can focus on the twins."

"Would you? That would help me out. As much as I love those babies, taking care of them for twelve hours is challenging."

Erica chuckled. "It's hard enough dealing with one. I have to admit, though, I miss those days. I'd love to have another baby."

"The wedding's coming up soon. You never know—maybe next year you and Dalton will end up having twins of your own."

"Don't say that! I said another baby. As in one. Not plural."

Reagan laughed.

"Enough about me," Erica said. "Where are you at with the shop?"

Her happy toes curled in dismay. Even the fuzziness of the socks felt rougher than they had a moment ago.

"Um…"

"Look, Reag, I applaud you for helping Marc and Brooke. They need it. But I don't want you to lose sight of why you're here. All of the forms and registrations and paperwork have to get done before you can even think about opening the store. And you need to get a contractor over there pronto."

"I know, I know." She sat up, accidentally spilling a few drops of tea on her pajama top.

She tried to think of what to say as she dabbed at the spill. Her sister had never understood her thought process. She didn't really understand it herself.

"I have the links for the state," Erica continued. "I'll text them to you. It's not hard to register your company name."

Registering a company name wasn't hard for Erica. Reagan was well aware that her sister thrived on that sort of thing. So why was it so hard for her? It didn't matter. If Erica had the links, she'd take them.

"Thanks, Erica. I actually do need that information."

"No problem. If you need help figuring everything out, I'm here. In fact, maybe I should come over soon." It wasn't the words Erica said. It was her tone. Skeptical of her little sister.

"I'm handling it."

"Are you?"

"Why would you ask that?" Annoyance flared. "You know I was at city hall to talk to the building inspector yesterday morning. If I hadn't been there, I wouldn't have found out about Brooke. And I did some research and took notes today, too." Putting her thoughts in circles always seemed to unblock her. As for the research? Very little was achieved.

"Let me guess. You wrote things in circles."

Reagan wasn't even responding. Just because the rest of her family lived by lists didn't mean she operated the same way. Lists jammed up her mind and confused her.

"It helps me see the big picture." Why was she even justifying herself? She didn't need to explain anything. This was her business. Her life.

"Well, don't lose sight of all the little details that make up the big picture. There's a lot to do."

Like she didn't know that.

"Oh, and, Reagan, you might want to call McCaffrey Construction to come out and give you an estimate on remodeling the building. We used them for the Winston, and Ed did a great job."

She perked up at that info. Why hadn't she thought to ask Erica who she'd hired to tackle the event center's renovations? Sometimes her thoughts felt like fifty butterflies in a flower garden. All of them fluttering away in a different direction. "Thank you. I will call him. But, listen, I really am getting things done for the chocolate shop. You don't have to worry. I've got this."

But did she? Sketching out a bare-bones circle diagram and reading through Wyoming's Department of Agriculture website to figure out if she needed a state food license—she still had no idea—before Marc had walked through the door tonight could hardly qualify as making progress.

"Just don't get distracted, okay? I love you, and I want you to succeed."

"I'm not distracted. I'm babysitting. They need my help."

"And you're wonderful to give it to them. You have the biggest heart, Reag. But I don't want it to get you into trouble. This chocolate shop is your dream."

"It is, and I'm going to make it happen. Now, please, no more lectures."

"But I'm your big sister. It's my job to lecture."

"I'm twenty-eight. All grown up."

Erica sighed. "You got me. I don't mean to come on too strong. I just… I love you. I want you to be happy. I want you to be happy *here*, you know?"

"Yeah, I do know, and you don't have to worry about it. I'm going to love it here."

Reagan asked about Rowan, and they discussed the wedding for a while before ending the call. Then she went into the kitchen and heated up another cup of tea. Erica seemed to think she was distracted. Was she? Reagan gave the kitchen a once-over and concluded that, yes, she was distracted.

There was so much to do, and it all demanded her attention. Take this house. She'd unpacked most of her stuff last week. But she really needed to go shopping. Now that she was living on her own, there were things she lacked. New curtains for the living room, a set of pans—the one skillet and small saucepan she owned weren't going to cut it—accessories for the bathroom, decorative items...

Reagan fought her rising anxiety as she held her mug with the steam wreathing into the air. The house needed her. The building needed her. The twins needed her.

At least decorating the house could wait. Except for the color of the walls, the kitchen was perfect. U-shaped with a window above the sink, it had cabinets painted a creamy white, butcher-block countertops and taupe walls. The taupe had to go. She was thinking a nice periwinkle blue.

Marc's kitchen had a cozy country feel. His mom probably had decorated it. It was too feminine for a cowboy to have picked out. The cabinets were natural wood, but the walls were a pale sage green and all of the accessories had rose-colored accents in floral patterns. She loved how comfortable, how vintage and how pretty it was.

That was what she wanted in this house. For it to be comfortable and pretty.

Erica seemed to think she had to get everything done for the business and her house in the next twenty-four hours. But Reagan wanted to enjoy this time. She wanted to go at her own pace. Decorate her house, get the forms and licenses done one by one and take care of the twins until Brooke could come home.

Her phone chimed, and she saw the links Erica had promised. One less thing she had to figure out on her own.

She took her mug over to the couch and settled a throw across her lap. She couldn't help but think how fortunate she was to be able to sit on her own couch in her own house with her own cup of tea. Poor Brooke was stuck in a hospital far away from her babies.

And poor Marc. He had his hands full. Calving was hard enough on a rancher. Taking care of infant twins, too? Making the hour-and-a-half drive to Casper to visit his sister each day? None of it was easy.

That was why earlier she'd gone over to him, hugged him and rubbed the muscles straining in his back. He'd looked so tired and lost. She'd wanted to take away some of his burdens and let him know he wasn't alone.

She still couldn't believe she'd prayed for Marc out loud. So unlike her.

It seemed impossible that she could have

comforted and prayed for the man she'd found so abrasive just over a week ago. But that was how life went. First impressions weren't always accurate. She hadn't known about his family troubles at the time.

And now that she did know?

She understood him a little better. Could see he was the protective type.

But that didn't mean she could grow close to him. She couldn't let his good looks and skills with the babies go to her head. The only man for her would put her first, not second-guess her decisions. She had no idea if Marc was capable of that. She'd just have to guard her heart. It was the safest thing to do.

Chapter Five

Looked like he'd found another one.

Thursday afternoon, Marc stopped the UTV far enough away to keep the cattle calm. A black calf was squirming on the ground in front of its mama, and they were already bonding as the mother licked it. A good sign. It was the second calf he'd found today. Grabbing his gear, he got out and approached the pair. The mother didn't like him near her newborn, but he quickly tagged the calf and made sure it could get to its feet. The little guy ran off to nurse.

Thank You, Lord, for another healthy calf. It made his job much easier when the cows and calves did what they instinctively knew to do.

He finished up and got back in the UTV to continue checking all of the places the cows liked to wander off to when having their babies.

Once he'd done a full sweep of the pastures, he drove back to the barn and parked.

Only then did Marc check his phone again. There were several texts from his mom. He ignored them for the moment. She'd been texting him all morning about the bakery and if he could make sure Deb had made the apple fritters and did he think sales would suffer if there were no pies this week? He'd responded that Deb knew what she was doing. More texts had landed. Mom asking him to bring more clothes and specifying exactly what items to bring, going so far as to tell him to take a picture of the shirts and jeans so she could make sure they were the right ones. He'd refused. It had gone on and on.

The new texts were more of the same. He replenished the calving supplies in the UTV before striding to his office. He kept reminding himself that his mom had been through a traumatic shock. This was her way of coping.

After logging the new calf's tag, he hiked down the path to the house and inhaled the crisp air. There was something about the in-between of winter and spring that spoke to him. Maybe it was simply the knowledge that warmer, brighter days were on their way.

He could use brighter days, that was for sure. At least the long drive to and from the hospital gave him time to clear his head. He didn't feel as frazzled when he could replay his list of ranch to-dos for the next day. As long as he didn't allow himself to think about Brooke's future or anything involving Reagan, he was fine.

Brooke's future was still uncertain, although she'd showed marked mental improvement yesterday. And Reagan? He was relying on her too much.

True to her word, she and Erica had created a volunteer list of babysitting teams to help watch the twins. Reagan would continue to drive to the ranch each morning and babysit until the volunteers arrived. He knew how tiring the twins were—he didn't want Reagan to get burned out. This schedule would free up her afternoons.

The first duo had been there last night when he'd gotten home from the hospital, and the next two weeks were covered. He hoped they wouldn't need help for two more weeks.

In the mudroom, he hung up his outerwear and continued through the kitchen to the living room. Reagan was kneeling on the quilted play mat with a bunny puppet in her hand, telling the babies a story. They were on their backs, staring up at her as if she were the most fascinating person on earth. He knew the feeling well.

"And then Betsy Bunny hopped over the fence," Reagan said in a silly voice as she made the puppet jump, "and landed right on a squishy frog."

Alice blew a raspberry in response, and Megan grasped her feet in the air.

Marc could have watched the three of them all day, but he really needed a shower. He stank. "How've they been today?"

"Great. As always." She grinned at the girls, scrunching her nose. "You two are the best babies in the world, aren't you?"

A longing bruised his heart. An unfamiliar longing. For this—a wife and child of his own. He hurried to the staircase, stumbling in the process. "I'll be back down in a few."

Reagan glanced over her shoulder, and her pretty eyes sparkled. "Have fun."

"I'll do my best." He gave her a cockeyed grin and took the stairs two at a time.

Twenty minutes later, he returned to the living room, feeling alive and clean in fresh jeans and a long-sleeved shirt. The babies were in carriers, drinking their bottles, and Alice looked asleep already. Megan was fighting to stay awake, but her eyelids kept drooping.

"Hey," he whispered, taking a seat on the couch.

"Hey," she whispered back with a smile. She took away Alice's bottle and placed a rolled-up receiving blanket under Megan's to prop it up. "She's almost out."

"I see that."

Reagan gracefully unfolded her legs to stand, then gave each foot a little kick before joining him on the other end of the couch. She looked tired. He didn't blame her.

"Any news on Brooke?" She kept her voice quiet as she gave him her full attention.

"Mom said she's much better cognitively." He glanced at Megan. She'd fallen asleep, too. What he wouldn't give to be able to stay right here for an hour or two. Rest his head against the couch and not think a single thought.

"That's good to hear. By the way, Marie Whitten and Leslie Grant are watching the twins later. Marie called to let me know they had supper for you. Baked ziti, salad, garlic bread and chocolate sheet cake."

His stomach growled just thinking about it.

"I appreciate all the trouble you and Erica went through to line up babysitters. And Mom wanted me to thank you for all the pictures of the girls. Brooke keeps asking about them, and the pictures are helping her keep it together."

"We should take the babies to see her." Reagan tugged the sleeve of her dark purple sweater down her wrist.

Take the babies all the way to the hospital?

Marc tried to think through the logistics of it. It would involve packing diaper bags, loading both car seats in his truck and driving a long distance with the girls. The whole thing gave him a headache. What if they cried? What would he do?

"She might be home in a few days." She wouldn't. Although the doctors had mentioned Brooke being discharged from the hospital in a few days if she showed enough improvement, they hadn't said a thing about her coming home. Everyone seemed to assume she'd be transferred to a rehab facility to continue physical therapy.

"You think so?" Reagan's nose scrunched. "I doubt she'll be home that soon. Even a week is an awfully long time for her to be away from the girls. I know you're busy, but what if I went with you on Saturday? The two of us should be able to handle getting the twins to her."

He massaged the back of his neck. Reagan was right, but he didn't want to deal with a long drive with three-month-old babies. Or with her. He owed her too much as it was. "I'll talk to my mom about it."

"Good."

"Ugh, where's my head at?" Rising, he jerked his thumb toward the staircase. "I forgot I needed to pack my mom some more clothes. I'll be right down."

Upstairs, he opened his mom's closet and found the items she'd requested. Once he'd folded them in a neat stack, a wave of exhaustion overcame him, and hoping it would subside, he perched on the edge of the bed.

He'd been doing so well, keeping his energy up, so why now was he sputtering on empty?

All he wanted to do was to curl up in his bed and take a twelve-hour nap. And when he woke up, he wanted Mom to be in the kitchen with a box of leftover donuts on the counter and Brooke taking care of the twins.

He wanted everything back to normal.

Knock, knock.

"Marc?" Reagan stood in the doorway.

"Yeah?" He got himself together and stood, grabbing the small pile of clothes in the process.

"Are you okay?"

"Yep."

"Have you been getting any sleep?"

"Sure. Why?" He didn't meet her eyes as he brushed past her to get to the hallway. He descended the staircase.

Reagan followed. "Why don't you rest for a little while?"

"Can't." He strode past the sleeping twins to the kitchen, where he rummaged through a cupboard to find an old grocery bag. Plucking one out, he shoved his mom's clothes into it.

"Thirty minutes. Just stretch out on your bed or the couch and close your eyes." She leaned her hip against the counter. "I'll set an alarm."

"Mom needs me. Brooke needs me. The girls need me. The cows need me. I don't have time for naps." His tone was too rough. Another thing to feel guilty about. Later. For now, he had to move. Just had to keep moving before he collapsed, before he fell apart.

Her hand on his arm halted him. He stared down at it. Short, groomed fingernails capped off long fingers. No polish. His gaze traveled up to her concerned face.

"The world won't end if you rest for half an hour. I promise."

He tossed the bag on the counter and braced his hands against the edge, letting his head drop. Then he glanced sideways at her. "Why do you care?"

"Because you're right. Brooke and your mom and the ranch and the twins need you. You won't be able to help anyone if you don't take care of yourself."

"I am taking care of myself."

"Okay." She brought her hands to her chest and backed up a step. "I'll shut up."

"I've got to go." He grabbed the bag and

gave her a lingering look. There was so much he wanted to say to her. To thank her for. He wanted to tell her he wasn't mad at her even though he was snarling. He wanted to tell her how much it touched him that she would give his well-being a second thought after spending hours taking care of the babies.

But the words wouldn't come and the clock was ticking.

"I'll see you tomorrow." He turned and left the room.

For the first time in a long time, he could admit to himself that his best wasn't good enough. Reagan deserved better than his bad mood. But it was all he had to give right now. And he doubted it was going to change anytime soon.

What a lousy afternoon. Frustrated, Reagan tossed her phone on her bed.

After Marc—clearly miffed at her suggestion that he get some rest—had blown her off, she'd gotten bottles ready and tidied the living room to prepare for Marie and Leslie. They'd arrived at three and assured her they'd be fine with the babies. Between them, they had seven kids—all grown—and thirteen grandchildren. She'd given them a quick tour and explained the girls' schedule as best as she could before they'd interrupted with personal questions.

"Do you have a boyfriend?"

"A chocolate shop, you say?"

"And you're living in town?"

"Raised in Wyoming?"

"Early service or late?"

By the time Leslie insisted Reagan meet her youngest son, Phil, who "might be a touch old for you, but you'll love him," Reagan was ready to sprint out the door.

And she basically had.

When she'd arrived home, she'd forced herself to call McCaffrey Construction. A receptionist took down her information and assured her Ed McCaffrey would call her back when he got a chance. Then she'd called the next contractor on the list only to have the man act like he was doing her a huge favor for even talking to her. His dismissive attitude and rude questions had made her stammer, and that had bothered her more than his tone.

Forget about it. She snatched up her phone, strode to the living room and laced her athletic shoes. Some fresh air would do her good.

Five minutes later, she found herself in front of her building. She tilted her head back and studied the brick with its ornamental stonework. The contractor's words from the phone call mocked her. "A former jewelry shop? You *do* realize you're going to have to add plumbing and electrical. We'll have to frame new walls. Sheetrock them and paint everything. It's not going to be a quick or easy project."

She'd responded with "I know," and he'd acted like she hadn't spoken. "Those old buildings usually need all new wiring and HVAC. There could be foundation issues. It'll be expensive."

If only she had retorted with "I'm not stupid. I know it's going to cost a lot of money. Do you want to give me an estimate or not?" But she hadn't. She'd simply listened to him drone on and on until he'd finally told her he'd get out there in a couple of weeks.

A couple—did that mean two? Three? More?

She really didn't want to work with anyone so dismissive and rude to her. For all she cared, he could lose her number permanently.

The air was still cold, and she burrowed her hands deeper into her coat pockets. If she went inside the building now, she'd start finding things wrong with it. Then she'd second-guess herself. She already doubted herself enough at the moment—not about making chocolates for a living—about little things. Like choosing the right contractor. Figuring out the links Erica had sent her. And if it had been a mistake to stick her nose in Marc's private life.

She hated making mistakes. Hated conflict even more. And as much as she liked being around the cowboy, she also knew allowing herself to get emotionally close to him would be a big mistake. He was too stubborn—conflict would be inevitable with a guy like him. And she'd be right where she'd been her entire life—backing down and doing things his way, the same as she'd done for years. She couldn't live like that anymore.

After one more glance at the building, she began to walk down the sidewalk toward the diner. With Marie and Leslie on duty at the ranch, she'd had no need to cook, and the thought of cooking for one tonight didn't excite her. Supper at Dixie B's it was.

Oof. Her body collided with someone. She stepped back and groaned. Of all the people to literally run into, Clem Buckley was the last person she'd choose.

"Watch where you're going, girly." He let out a huff, and those steely eyes pierced her all the way to her soul.

With a shaky inhalation, she attempted to get her nerves under control. "I'm sorry. I didn't see you there."

"I'm well aware of that." He narrowed his

eyes as he studied her face. "You ain't sick, are you? You look poorly."

Poorly. Yes, that was exactly how she felt.

"I'm not sick. I just have a lot on my mind."

He pulled back his shoulders and skewered her with a look full of doubt. It made her feel twitchy, like every nerve ending was about to fritz. She should excuse herself and move on, but no, it appeared she was rooted to the concrete sidewalk.

"You aren't about to cry, are you?" he asked.

Yes. She hadn't even realized it until he'd mentioned it.

"No." Her voice was squeaky. She tried to toughen up, but all she could muster was a melancholy sigh.

"Come on." Clem adjusted his cowboy hat and cocked his head to the side. "I can see you need sustenance. You'll feel better after a meal at Dixie B's."

Unexpected gratitude flooded her, making her feel even more off balance than she already was.

"I was just heading there," she said, sniffing. Oddly enough, she didn't mind the thought of eating with Clem. It beat eating alone. "You don't have to come with me."

"I know I don't have to. But someone has to make sure you eat. You need to get some meat on your bones." He started striding toward the diner. She caught up to him and matched his pace. "Don't go making a fuss about it, either, girly. I don't do tears, and I don't do nonsense."

No tears. No nonsense. Got it.

Reagan remained silent the three blocks it took to get there, and when Clem opened the door for her, she gave him a genuine smile before entering the diner. Straight ahead, a row of booths against the wall was filled with hungry families. Tables of four lined the center of the room, and a counter with built-in stools was off to the left. Framed pictures of families and wildlife hung on the forest-green walls.

Clem guided her to the only empty booth near the back. Customers greeted him along the way, and he acknowledged everyone who did. He took the bench facing the front of the restaurant, and she slid into the bench opposite him. Laminated menus stuck out between the wall and the salt and pepper shakers. She took one and opened it.

The warm air carried conversations punctuated with laughter and the smell of chicken soup and French fries. She wasn't all that hungry. Whenever her mind was troubled, her appetite tended to disappear.

"Well, hey there, Clem. Who's this you got with you?" A smiling, curvy woman in her thirties stopped by their table. She was wearing a maroon T-shirt with the Dixie B's logo on it, jeans and an apron. Her dark brown hair was pulled back in a ponytail, revealing a dragonfly tattoo behind her ear.

"Molly, this is Reagan—" he turned his attention to Reagan "—what's your last name, again?"

"Mayer." She smiled at Molly. "Reagan Mayer."

"Oh, right," Molly said, pointing her pen to Reagan. "You're helping out with Brooke's babies, aren't you? We all feel so bad for Miss Anne and Brooke."

"Yes." Reagan shifted her gaze to the menu. It wasn't only Anne and Brooke suffering. "And for Marc."

Molly continued as if she hadn't said anything. "Deb's been asking around for help at the bakery, but we all can only do so much, you know? I spent a few hours there yesterday, but Tag didn't have preschool this morning, and I don't have a babysitter, so—"

"We're ready to order." Clem's firm tone stopped Molly in her tracks. Her sideways glare blasted disapproval.

"Right." Molly's cheer was gone, replaced by a wooden expression. "Go on, then."

"Ladies first." Clem nodded to Reagan.

"I'll have a bowl of your chicken noodle soup."

"Anything else?"

"No."

"What to drink?" Molly looked up from her notepad and pen.

"Do you have lemonade?"

"We sure do." Molly turned to Clem. "And you?"

"Bring her a BLT on grilled sourdough, too." He addressed Molly, then faced Reagan. "Unless you're vegetarian."

"I'm not a vegetarian. But I don't need—"

He'd already dismissed her. "Bring the BLT. I'll have the Reuben, fries and an iced tea. No lemon."

She gave them a curt nod. "Be back in a few with your drinks."

Reagan was about to tell him she wasn't that hungry, but he spoke up before she could. "What's troubling you, girly?"

Put like that... "It's nothing. I mean, it's not nothing... I don't know where to begin."

"Start somewhere."

It was on the tip of her tongue to mention Erica and how organized she was and how inferior Reagan felt compared to her in that department, but this was Clem. No tears, no nonsense Clem.

She picked up her napkin and began twisting it. "You see, chocolate? I understand. Running a

business? I can do that, too. For the most part."
She was confident in her abilities to make the
chocolate, order supplies and package orders.
The website designer she and her mother had
used for their company had agreed to design
hers when she was ready. And Mom had been
the one to suggest linking R. Mayer Chocolates'
online store with the Mayer Canyon Candles'
website. "But getting the permits and renovations done? That, I don't understand."

"What do you need to do?" he asked.

"I don't know. Everything." Molly arrived
with their drinks, and Reagan thanked her.

"You met with Henry?" He ripped the paper
off his straw and dunked the straw into his iced
tea.

"Tried to. He was running late, and I ended
up meeting with Marc Young instead, but we
were interrupted when his sister collapsed."

"Right, right." He nodded. "Where are you
stuck?"

"I'm not sure." She already felt less anxious
sitting here and talking to Clem, of all people.
"My sister sent me links to register the business
with the state, but I didn't understand everything. And I couldn't figure out the Department
of Ag website at all. Do I need a food license
or not? And how do I get one? Erica has mentioned banking and getting some sort of num-

ber, and I don't think I can even apply for one until I get the other stuff done. Today I called two contractors… That didn't go well."

"Sounds to me you bit off more than you can chew."

The lemonade soured on her tongue. Even Clem knew she wasn't capable of doing all this.

"But—" he pointed his finger to her "—it's fixable."

It was? "How?"

"My buddy Slim Nixon retired a few years ago. He's started several businesses and spent a decade on the board of the chamber of commerce. He knows how to do everything you mentioned. I can give him a call and, for a fee—he doesn't work for free, girly—I'm sure he'd help you get everything done."

It was as if the clouds had parted and the sunlight was shining right on her face.

She could hire someone to help her.

Her mouth curved upward. Why hadn't she thought of this?

"You really think he'd help me?"

"I can ask." One of his shoulders lifted. "I have a feeling he'll want to help you."

"Why? He doesn't know me."

"Fellas like me? We get bored. Need a challenge now and then."

Their food arrived, and Reagan couldn't believe the portion sizes. The bowl of soup could feed three people, and the BLT had to have a pound of bacon piled on it.

"Eat up." He picked up his Reuben and gestured to her with it before taking a big bite.

She dipped the spoon into her soup and glanced up at him. "Thanks, Clem. I needed this."

"I know." He wiped his mouth with a napkin. "The protein will fill you up."

"No, not the food—although it looks delicious—the help. Thank you."

"Bah." He waved her off. "It's nothing."

"It's not nothing. I appreciate it."

"Well, don't go blubbering about it. Eat your food."

No use in arguing about that. Her mood had completely shifted. She suddenly had an appetite. Clem had chased away the doom cloud hanging over her. He'd get in touch with Slim and, in the meantime, she'd relax.

Now she could babysit the twins tomorrow without tying herself into knots about making progress on her business during their naptime. And if Marc agreed to take the babies to see Brooke on Saturday, she wouldn't feel guilty about helping him with that, either.

She was doing this for the twins and Brooke, not for Marc. Yes, there was a connection there.

But he wasn't the guy for her. She wanted someone who valued her opinion and listened to her. He might be attractive and protective, but she needed more than looks, needed more than a protective cowboy. She needed someone who understood her. Marc didn't, and she doubted he could.

Chapter Six

Marc was starting the day off right—with a cup of coffee and an apology to Reagan. She should be here within ten minutes. He held Megan in one arm as he poured himself a cup and took it back to the living room, where Alice was fussing in her carrier. Megan had been on the verge of wailing before he'd picked her up. And look at her now...happy as could be.

"I know, I know, kiddo. Uncle Marc's back." He set the mug on a coaster and proceeded to strap Megan into her bouncy seat. Then he scooped up Alice and held her close. "See? Nothing to cry about. I've got you. I'll always be here for you."

She gurgled in reply and he kissed her forehead. Then he settled her in the bouncy seat next to her sister, sank into the couch and took his first sip of coffee. Pure bliss. He set down the mug and closed his eyes for a moment.

It had been a long night. The girls had woken up at three, as usual, and as soon as they'd had their bottles, he'd put them back to bed. As he'd dragged himself, bleary-eyed, to his own bedroom, a text had come through from Rico that he'd found a newborn calf with no mama around.

Normally, Marc would throw on a coat and drive out to the pasture where Rico had found the calf, but he couldn't. Couldn't just leave the twins in the house alone. Rico had taken the calf back to the barn and cared for it, but Marc hadn't been able to sleep as all the scenarios ran through his head. He'd finally dozed off about an hour before the twins were up for good. Fifteen minutes ago, Rico had updated him—he'd found the mother cow. He'd keep an eye on the pair until Marc was able to get out there.

If he wasn't so tired, he'd reach over and take another drink of the coffee. Maybe he just needed to sit here, eyes closed, for a few minutes. Get his bearings. Prepare for another long day…

"Marc?"

Something pushed against his shoulder.

"Marc?"

He opened one eye, then the other and stared into Reagan's golden-brown ones. "There you are."

Where was he supposed to be?

"Don't get mad." Reagan held Alice and backed up a few steps. Then she bent and un-buckled Megan. She managed to make picking up Megan while holding Alice look effortless. A baby in each arm and a smile on her face. His gut clenched. He'd never met anyone like Reagan.

"Why would I be mad?" The words sounded like they'd been tossed in gravel. He cleared his throat and glanced over at the mug sitting nearby. The coffee. He grabbed it and took a sip—ice-cold. How long had he been out?

"When I came in, you were resting, and I didn't want to wake you, so..." She gave him a small shrug.

He jerked to attention. The calf. Rico. The twins.

"I got here twenty minutes ago," she said in a singsong voice as she made faces to each of the girls. "And you looked so peaceful, I let you be. I know you need to get out to the cows, so I finally woke you up. Yes, I did, didn't I?"

Megan grabbed a lock of Reagan's hair and promptly shoved it in her mouth. "You don't want that. Yucky." She laughed and glanced at Marc. "Could you take my hair out of her hand? I would, but..."

"Your hands are full." He stood and gently

pried open Megan's fist to release the hair. Then he pushed the tendrils behind Reagan's ear. He tried not to think about how soft it felt or the feminine fragrance that lingered. He stepped away. "I'm sorry about yesterday."

"No worries."

"I mean it. I was short with you, and I feel bad about it."

"You're under a lot of stress."

"It doesn't excuse it."

"I know, but it really isn't a big deal."

He met her gaze, and he felt bad at the vulnerability lurking in there. She'd been so kind to him. He hated that he'd been rude.

"Did you talk to your mom about taking the twins to visit Brooke tomorrow?"

"I did." His mom had burst into tears right then and there. "I thought I had upset her because she started crying. But she was relieved. She misses the twins and thinks it will do Brooke a world of good to see them."

"And Brooke? Does she know?"

"Yes. When we told her about it, she said she was going to work extra hard with the therapist so she could try to hold them."

"Do you think she'll be able to?"

"One at a time. If we hand the baby to her. She's able to lift her arm and move her fingers, but the strength isn't there for much more than that."

"I'm sorry."

"I am, too." He caressed Alice's head. "The good news is that the doctors assure us that, with therapy, they think she'll make a full recovery. She's sharp—not slurring her words anymore—and the therapists are starting to see noticeable improvement in her left side. The doctors are running tests today to see if she could be released soon."

"To come home?"

"I'm not sure. I don't see how she could come home with her arm and leg still so weak. But maybe."

"What time do you want to go tomorrow?" Reagan shifted Alice to grip her better.

"If we left around nine, would that work? Then we could be back by early afternoon."

"Sure."

"I have to figure out the car seats. I don't know how to get them in the truck."

"Why not take her minivan?"

He smacked his forehead. "Why didn't I think of that?"

"Because you're thinking about a million other things." She bent to lay Megan on the play mat, set Alice next to her and reached over to the toy basket to grab toys for each of the girls.

"Yeah, I guess." He should head out and relieve Rico, but this time with Reagan was a reprieve from everything. "I never asked if you were able to talk with Henry or not."

"I wasn't. I need to reschedule our meeting." She gestured to the kitchen. "Mind if I grab a cup of coffee before you take off?"

"Not at all." He felt like a traitor for even mentioning Henry. Wasn't he supposed to be on his mom's side in all this? The building, the bakery—he couldn't muster up an ounce of energy about either at the moment. But Reagan... yeah, he could muster up energy for her. He wanted her to be happy. Just not at his mother's expense.

As soon as she was out of sight, anxiety rushed through him. He should have been out at the barn half an hour ago. There were cows to check. Chores to be done. Tonight he'd have to pack the girls' diaper bag for tomorrow, and he'd never done that before. Would he need to keep their bottles refrigerated? Bring a cooler? He almost hung his head. Taking the babies out of the house was new to him. And scary.

"Here, I figured you needed one, too." Reagan handed him a mug. Everything about her seemed to shine. She was open and easy, and he wished he could talk to her about the many things on his mind. How he worried about each pregnant cow and newborn calf. And how scared he was that his sister would be disabled for the rest of her life. Then there was his mom. He needed to explain to Reagan why her building was so important to his mother.

But it wouldn't be fair to burden Reagan with that, not when the building was important to her, too.

Unwanted memories crept up on him. Of his mother's haggard face the day she had come home and announced she'd leased a building in town to open a bakery. She'd tried to look cheerful, but he'd known how difficult that step had been for her. More than once, she'd joked that her bakery was the ugly duckling of Jewel River. Easily passed over. Too small to notice.

"Thanks." He accepted the mug and took a sip. *Come on, man, leave. Walk out the door. You have responsibilities.* "How are you settling into your house?"

She blinked rapidly and took a drink. "I have a lot of shopping to do. And painting."

"I'd offer to help paint..."

Her laugh brightened the room. "I think you have enough on your plate as it is."

"Yeah, I do."

"Dalton and Erica are going to help. I have no idea when. I haven't picked out colors or anything. By the way, I ran into Clem Buckley yesterday afternoon."

"Oh, yeah? Did he frighten any children?"

"No," she said, grinning. "He's been very helpful. He has a friend who might guide me through the process of filling out all my business paperwork."

He actually felt his face crumble. This conversation needed to be handled correctly without him being a jerk about it. He forced a smile on his face. "Any chance you'd want to check out the other empty buildings Jewel River has to offer?"

Her golden eyes darkened as the corners of her mouth pinched. "I don't think so. I've already got the right one."

They sat there staring at each other, sipping their coffees and pretending this obstacle wasn't a problem. But they both knew it was.

"Well, I'd better get out there." He stood.

"Yep. I'll see you later. Mary and Bill Steyn will be here later. They're bringing pizza."

"Great." Marc wanted to thaw the ice between them, but he didn't know how. "Thanks again. Text me if you need anything."

He was heading to the kitchen when he heard her soft voice say, "I won't."

I won't. His step almost faltered. He deserved

it. All he'd done was take from her, and he couldn't even be supportive of her new venture.

It was better this way. Reagan's personality drew him to her. He wanted to get closer to her, but he couldn't. He didn't have room in his life—or his heart—for anything more. The women who needed him had all of him already.

"This afternoon?" Reagan frowned as she kept an eye on the twins, still napping in their carriers on the living room floor, while she talked to Ed McCaffrey. She hadn't expected him to call back so soon or want to meet her at the building today.

"Yes, I'm going to be out that way anyhow. We might as well do a walk-through, and you can fill me in on what you want done."

She hesitated.

"If this afternoon doesn't work for you," Ed said, "it will have to wait until the week after next. I'm booked out."

"I'll meet you there today. Can you give me an hour?"

"That works for me. I look forward to seeing you there." He ended the call.

Reagan frowned at the phone. This changed things. She scurried over to her tote bag and took out the folder with her notes. She'd been jotting down ideas as they came to her, and she wanted to make sure she didn't miss anything when she talked to Ed.

Before leaving Denver, she'd asked Oliver, the owner of the chocolate shop, what his must-haves were for a building, and he'd rattled off a number of things she wouldn't have thought of on her own. Where had she put the paper with his ideas? She flipped through the pages in the folder twice before she found it. After giving it a quick skim, she clicked a pen and jotted down a few more thoughts.

Earlier, she'd texted Erica to let her know Marc had agreed to take the babies to the hospital tomorrow. Should she text her again to ask her to join her at the building for the meeting with Ed? It would be good to have another set of ears and eyes there in case she missed anything. But what if Erica and Ed felt one way about something and she felt another? Would they team up against her? Make her doubt her choices?

It was a chance she was willing to take. She called Erica.

"Hey, Reag, what's up?"

"Ed McCaffrey is meeting me at the building in an hour. Any chance you'd want to join us there?" She held her breath as she waited for her answer.

"I can't. I'm dropping off Rowan to Jamie's early. Want me to see if Dalton can come out?"

"No, that's okay." She could handle this. Couldn't she?

"By the way, Dalton contacted Marc about going over there to check his cattle tomorrow. He figured if Marc was in Casper with you, he'd need the extra help."

"Really?" This was why she adored her sister. "That is so thoughtful of you guys."

"Marc would do the same if Dalton needed help."

She didn't doubt it. He seemed the type of cowboy who would step in at a moment's notice to help anyone...unless it was her.

It would have been nice to have the type of friendship where she could ask Marc to join her for the contractor meeting. He'd made it abundantly clear, though, he still wanted his mother to have her building. Therefore, he would be no help to her.

"Let me know if you change your mind about Dalton joining you."

"I'll be fine." After the call was over, Reagan was faced with a choice. Did she meet Ed alone? Or did she call someone else to join her? Clem would. She had no doubt. But that would bring up even more issues she wasn't prepared to deal with.

No, it was time to handle her business. She'd meet Ed alone and hope she didn't forget to mention anything important. She also hoped he wouldn't make her feel like a three-year-old attempting quantum physics.

Reagan checked on the twins again. Still sleeping, the sweethearts. A knock on the front door alerted her that Mary and Bill had arrived.

After chatting with the quiet couple for a few minutes and explaining what the twins needed, Reagan drove to town and parked in front of her building. As she got out of her vehicle, a truck pulled in next to her. A man in his midsixties got out, adjusted his cowboy hat and stared up at the building. She joined him on the sidewalk.

"Hi, I'm Reagan Mayer." She held out her hand. He gave it a vigorous shake. The cheer in his eyes put her at ease. He reminded her of her father. Trustworthy and solid.

"Ed McCaffrey. Let's see what you've got here." He hitched his thumb to the entrance. He held an iPad and notepad under one arm. "This here's a beauty. You're Erica's sister, right?"

"Yes. I moved here a few weeks ago."

"Well, she has a good eye for detail. The Winston is coming along fine."

"She does. My sister is nothing if not thorough." Reagan unlocked the door, and he held it open for her to enter first. Inside, she flipped on the lights.

"I have to admit, it's been some time since I've been in here. My wife left me long ago, so I didn't have a need for jewelry." The smile lines around his eyes emphasized his playful tone. "You're converting this into a chocolate shop, correct?"

"Correct." She set her tote and purse on the front counter and took out the folder with her notes. Her fingers trembled slightly. *Stop it. You don't have to be nervous.*

"How soon do you want it opened? Do you have a deadline in mind?"

"Um…not really. I figured it would depend on how long the renovations would take."

"Let's see what we've got." He nodded, booting up the iPad. Then he took out a tape measure from his pocket.

For the next thirty minutes, Reagan followed Ed around the entire interior and answered his questions to the best of her ability.

"It looks like the electrical wiring and ductwork was all replaced in the early nineties. That's what I'm guessing, at least. Probably when Dewey bought the place. I do recommend replacing the furnace and air-conditioning unit since they're well past their prime. If you want to hold off, though, I understand. That leaves reconfiguring the floor plan to add the work area, a small kitchen, a break room and remodeling the bathroom and office. New floors throughout, fresh paint on the walls. We'll install the climate-controlled display cases, but you're in charge of ordering them. Now, how many tables do you plan on having up here?" Ed pointed to the entrance area.

"Tables?" What did he mean?

"You know, for people to sit."

"Oh, I'm not having a sitting area. No tables."

"Gotcha." He scratched his chin. "What are you going to do with the space, then?" He checked his notes. "I am correct that all of these displays are being taken out, right?"

"Yes, you're correct." Reagan bit her lower lip as it hit her how much empty space there would be up front.

"There's no crime in having some room to breathe." He smiled warmly. "And if you change your mind, you could easily fit several tables up there for customers."

She didn't know how to respond, so she remained silent.

"I'll work up an estimate for you next week."

"When would you be available to start the work?" She followed him to the front door, where he was staring up at the ceiling. Then he poked his finger along a piece of chipped paint on the door frame and made another note on his notepad.

"My crew will get started as soon as the building permit is issued. I'm sure you're eager to open your shop, so we'll work it in around our other projects." He pointed to the corner of the ceiling. "I'm adding a new alarm system to the quote. You want to be safe."

"About the building permit… What do I need to do to get one?" She clasped her hands, wringing them tightly. Her pulse was beating too fast. She dreaded having to deal with the permit.

"Leave that to me. I'll take care of all that for you. I work with Henry all the time."

"You will?" Could she hire him on the spot?

"I will. Okay, then, Reagan. I'll get this estimate to you next week. You have yourself a fine weekend, and welcome to Jewel River. I'm looking forward to trying some of those chocolates."

"Thank you for coming out here today. You've been a big help."

They said goodbye and Ed left. As Reagan gathered her things, hope chased away all her worries.

This was really going to happen. She had a great feeling about hiring McCaffrey Construction to tackle the renovation. Now, if she could get Slim to help her with the other paperwork, she'd be in shape to open the shop this summer. That meant…it was finally time to tackle the fun stuff.

She could start ordering all the equipment she needed to open the store.

After spinning in a pirouette, she grabbed her tote and purse, hiked them onto her shoulder and locked up the building. Meeting with Ed had been the breakthrough she'd needed.

The life she'd been dreaming about would be reality soon.

Chapter Seven

Marc finally loosened his grip on the mini-van's steering wheel midway through the drive to the hospital. He and Reagan had gotten a later start than expected. Alice had needed a complete outfit change after a major diaper blowout, and Reagan had taken one look at the bottles Marc had prepared and announced there weren't enough. She was right, of course, and she'd made additional bottles while he'd taken care of the diaper. Reagan had definitely gotten the better end of the deal on that one.

"Did you grow up in Jewel River?" Reagan asked as she adjusted the heat. They'd worked through a number of topics so far, including Dalton checking the calves for him and what to expect at the hospital.

"I did. Right on the ranch, too."

"Your mother has a house in town, right? I

mean, I know she's living with you now...but that's to help with the twins. Or is it permanent?"

"Temporary." He hoped so, at least. Not because he had anything against his mother, but he wanted her life to get back to normal. She loved her house in town, loved being so close to the bakery. If Brooke needed more care, what would that mean for the twins? For his mom?

"I know I'm being nosy, so don't feel like you have to answer, but why doesn't she live on the ranch? It's hers, right?"

"Not anymore."

"Is it yours?"

"Yeah. After my father left us, he filed for divorce and wanted his portion of the ranch assets. Mom ended up selling a lot of acreage to help pay his settlement. We couldn't afford a full-time cowboy anymore, and I took over running the ranch while she opened the bakery. Several years ago, we agreed it made sense for me to buy the ranch from her." What he didn't mention was how touch and go the finances were those first years. If it wasn't for the bakery, they might have lost the ranch altogether.

"How old were you when your father left?"

"Sixteen." He'd trained himself to feel detached, but moments like this made all his dormant emotions rise to the surface. Maybe it was the fact Reagan was the one asking. She wasn't just making idle chitchat. She actually cared.

"And you took over the ranch by yourself? You were young. Still in high school. I can't imagine how you managed it all."

"We still had a cowboy for a short time after my father left since the divorce took a while to finalize. I was able to graduate early from high school so I could concentrate on the cattle."

"Sounds like you had to grow up quick."

He shrugged, giving her a small smile. "Yeah, well, it worked out all right. Mom isn't interested in ranching, and I am. I took out a mortgage to buy the ranch from her, and she used the money to pay off the loans she'd taken out for the bakery. She hired a financial advisor to set up a retirement plan, and best of all, she was able to buy her house. She loves that house."

The past five years had been profitable for him, too. He'd paid down the mortgage and refinanced at a lower rate. His finances were in the best shape they'd ever been.

"My mom isn't into ranching, either, although she always lends a helping hand if needed." Reagan peeked at him through shy eyes. "Do you ever see your father?"

"No, I haven't seen or heard from him since the divorce." It hurt saying it out loud. Hurt thinking about it, too. Marc was older now, but knowing his father didn't want to be part of his life still stung.

"I'm sorry. That must be difficult. Painful."

"I survived."

"You more than survived. You've succeeded under very tough circumstances."

Her compliment seeped inside him, made him want to savor it. He'd done what he'd had to do. But it had been hard.

She turned to check on the babies. They'd stopped babbling ten minutes ago. "They're asleep."

"Good. They'll be fresh for Brooke." He checked the rearview and switched lanes. "So you grew up on a ranch, too, huh?"

"Yep. Mayer Canyon Ranch. I have two older brothers—Jet and Blaine—and they divided the ranch between them after my dad retired. My parents wanted everything to be fair, so Erica and I get a small percentage of the profits, and we each have a parcel of land on the property if we ever want to build a home. My other brother, Cody, died in a car accident several years ago."

Her tone toward the end matched the one he'd used for his father—detached. "Were you close to Cody?"

She nodded, staring straight ahead. "Yes, I was." Each word was softer than the previous one.

"I'm sorry he died."

"I am, too."

The atmosphere had grown melancholy. He couldn't stand it. "Tell me how you came to own a candle business."

"My mom started making candles as a hobby when I was in high school, and I thought it looked fun. So we did it together, and before you know it, we were selling them. Dad told us we should convert one of the old pole barns into a workshop, and we did. Erica set up the business. She's great at that. And Mom and I made the candles. I loved coming up with new scents."

"You're really creative." It wasn't a question. It was a fact. He'd seen her telling stories to the twins. It didn't surprise him one bit that she would come up with new scents. Her chocolates would probably be delicious. As unique as she was, too.

"Thank you. I wouldn't mind having some of Erica's organizational skills, too, though. My way of doing things positively terrifies her."

"As long as it works for you, who cares?"

Her mouth opened then closed as she stared at him and frowned.

"What? Did I say something wrong? I wasn't trying to offend you."

"No, no." She turned her attention to the view out her window. "My family really doesn't get how I do things, and they have strong opinions about how I should do them. Well, everyone except my brother Blaine. He's pretty supportive."

He chuckled. "Let me guess. They don't do things the way you do?"

"Bingo." Her smile made her face even prettier than it already was. "I've been second-guessing myself for a long time."

"At some point, they'll recognize that you've figured life out."

"Maybe after I actually have figured life out…"

"Why do you say that?" Her self-effacement took him by surprise. "Are you having second thoughts about the chocolate shop?"

"You wish." She grinned.

He flashed her a surprised look, but at the mischief twinkling in her eyes, he relaxed.

"For the record," he said, "I have nothing against your shop beyond the location."

"I know." She settled back into her seat. "No, I'm confident about opening the store. I met with a contractor yesterday. It went much better than I'd expected. And I'm starting to get excited about ordering all the equipment I'll need. I really miss being able to experiment with the flavors. I had this idea for a cinnamon caramel that I just know people will love…"

As he listened to her talk about the chocolates and the decorating skills she'd learned using edible paint, his entire body relaxed. There was something soothing about hearing her obvious enthusiasm for making the candy.

All too soon, he was navigating the minivan through the city streets to the parking lot of the hospital. When he parked the van, he turned to Reagan. "Thank you. I couldn't have made this trip without you. In fact, I wouldn't have even considered it. I don't know what it's going to be like in there. My mom...she's usually the most welcoming person you could ever meet, but..." He didn't know how she'd react to Reagan, and he wanted his mom to like her.

Reagan placed her hand on his arm. "It's okay. She probably hasn't slept more than a few hours at a time all week, and you all still need answers about Brooke. Don't worry. I can handle this."

He was glad someone could handle it. Because he wasn't sure he could.

"Do you think we should feed them first?" she asked.

"Nah, let's get them into the double stroller. If they're hungry, Mom will help us feed them. She is probably having baby withdrawals after this week."

"Good point."

Marc got out and opened the back hatch to unfold the stroller. Reagan exited the minivan and slid open the side door. Marc rolled the stroller to her. "Here, let me."

He popped Megan's seat out of its base and locked it into where it fit in the stroller. Then he wheeled around to the other side and repeated the process with Alice's seat. The girls made noises like they were waking up.

"Are you ready for this?" He had a firm grip on the stroller. She hiked the straps of the diaper bag and her purse up on her shoulder and nodded. "Okay. Let's go."

They headed to the entrance, through the sliding glass doors and straight to the bank of elevators in the hall. Marc pressed the number for Brooke's floor and tried to ignore the acid in his stomach. Would seeing the twins be hard on Brooke since she couldn't be with them? Would the doctors have a plan for her release? Would his mom act weird with Reagan around?

Minutes later, they reached Brooke's door. With his nerves taut, he knocked. "We're coming in."

He pushed the door open and waited for Reagan to enter before propelling the stroller inside. Brooke, sitting up in the hospital bed, promptly burst into tears, and his mom jumped to her feet.

He wasn't sure what was happening. He glanced at Reagan, who smiled brightly as she set the diaper bag on the floor.

"The girls are here!" Mom didn't give him a second glance as she began to unbuckle Alice. She lifted the baby high in the air and kissed her cheeks again and again. Then she settled her against her chest and beamed at Marc. "Thank you, honey. These dears are a sight for sore eyes."

Reagan was unbuckling Megan, leaving Marc surprised that neither baby had started to cry. Yet. They'd just woken up and were hungry.

Reagan brought Megan over to Brooke, who held out her arms, although the left arm wasn't as high as the right. His sister was clearly trying to pull herself together. As Reagan gently laid the baby in her arms, Marc hurried to Brooke's side in case she needed help.

"I'll get her bottle." Reagan turned away to pull out two bottles from the bag. "I'll see if I can warm these up." She left the room.

"Oh, I've missed you, Meggie." Brooke held her in the crook of her right arm. She slowly brought her left hand to Megan's forehead. Marc was surprised she was able to lift her hand so high. She truly was making progress. "It's been too long since I've held you. Mom, will you bring Alice over so I can see her?"

His mother stood and brought the baby to Brooke. A fresh batch of tears dripped down his sister's cheeks. Marc looked around the room and found a box of tissues. Grabbing one, he handed it to Brooke, and he was glad to see she was able to dab her face with it using her left hand.

"You're really getting your strength back." He nodded to her hand. She reached out to him, and he took it. She squeezed it slightly.

"I am. I couldn't do that two days ago. The therapy is really helping."

"You should see her, Marc. All day long, she has occupational therapists and physical therapists coming to get her. She's working her tail off."

"It's exhausting." Brooke sounded tired, but her expression was full of love for Megan, settling deeper into her arms. "This morning we got some positive news."

"Yes," Mom interrupted with a worried glance to his sister. "Brooke is moving tomorrow."

"Moving?" Marc pictured bringing her back home. She seemed to still need a lot of care.

"There's a short-term rehab hospital nearby with a room for her. She'll be going there in the morning."

"That's great news." She'd improved enough to enter the next phase—good news indeed. "How long will you be there? And what kind of rehab are we talking?"

Brooke looked up from Megan to him. "Most people spend around three weeks there, but the doctor told me since I'm young and motivated, I could be home in a week or two."

His mom's smile was tender but concerned. "They told her to expect a minimum of three hours of work each day."

"Work? What kind of work?"

Brooke relaxed her head against the pillows. "Mostly physical therapy. I'm doing better walking. Haven't recovered full use of this hand, though."

"These should be warm." Reagan breezed back into the room and handed Brooke a bottle and his mom one. Mom sat in the chair again to feed Alice.

Two other chairs stood next to each other against the opposite wall, so he and Reagan sat in them. The only noises were the babies drinking their bottles and the beeps of the hospital.

"I should leave you alone. Give you some privacy." Reagan began to stand but Marc stopped her.

"I'm sorry—I forgot to introduce you. Mom, Brooke, this is Reagan Mayer. She just moved to Jewel River. Reagan, this is Brooke and my mother, Anne."

His mother's smile was full of gratitude. "Erica's sister. You've been so kind to us. I don't know where to begin. Thank you."

Brooke nodded, clearly choked up. "I was so

worried when I realized I'd been in the hospital for a few days. Mom showed me all the pictures you sent, and it was such a relief. I can't thank you enough for all you've done."

"It's my pleasure. I love babies, and I have the time to help right now."

"Knowing they're in good hands has been the most precious gift." Brooke looked ready to cry again, so Marc went over and took Megan from her.

"I'll burp her and give her right back," he said.

"Actually, will you bring Alice to me? I need to cuddle her, too."

"You got it."

"I'll bring her over," his mom said, rising.

Reagan found a burp cloth in the diaper bag and handed it to him. The expression in her eyes made him feel like they were a team, and he appreciated it. He'd been feeling so lost and on his own ever since he'd gotten the call from his mom about Brooke collapsing. He shifted the baby to his shoulder and softly patted her back.

"Brooke's moving to a short-term rehab center tomorrow," Marc told Reagan. "Isn't that great?"

"That's fantastic." She beamed. "Do you need anything? Clothes? Supplies?"

His mom settled Alice in Brooke's arms. "I'll take care of all that, Reagan. I plan on coming home tomorrow night. Then I'll drive here during the day and spend my nights at home this week. We'll see where things stand after that." His mom's cell phone rang. "I've got to take this." She hurried out of the room.

"Marc, what's going to happen with the babies while I'm at the rehab facility?"

"I'll keep watching them," Reagan said. "Don't worry about the girls."

"Reagan's great with the babies." Marc nodded. "You just worry about getting healthy and coming home, okay?"

"It's so much, though, asking you to watch them." Brooke's forehead wrinkled. "I can pay you."

Reagan's laugh tinkled in the air. "I don't want money. Trust me when I say spending time with two of the cutest babies in the world is payment enough."

"They are really cute, aren't they?" Brooke smiled.

"The cutest." Marc kissed the top of Megan's head.

His mom came back into the room. An air of dejection trailed behind her.

"What's wrong?" Marc asked.

"Deb can't work at the bakery tomorrow. She had an emergency—don't worry, she's fine— and says she'll be okay to work on Monday. But

I don't know what to do. I can't be there. I need to be here. There are a lot of moving parts involved with Brooke's transfer, and I don't want to miss any of it."

Marc's spirits dropped to the floor. Just when everything was improving, another thing had to go wrong. Why couldn't anything be easy for once?

"What about Jackie?" Marc asked.

Reagan kept quiet as she watched the exchange between him and his mother. For five minutes now, they'd been trying to work out a solution for the bakery. They both looked completely exhausted.

On the one hand, she was thrilled for Brooke to be moving from the hospital tomorrow. On the other hand, she could see the toll this week had taken on Anne. The woman clearly needed more sleep. Maybe even a week to sit on a couch, watch old movies, sip tea and do nothing else. It would help her tremendously.

"Jackie's out of town for the weekend." Anne seemed to be on the verge of tears, and Reagan got the impression this wasn't a woman who cried often—if ever.

"Who else knows how to make all of the pastries?" Marc's tone was patient. Reagan was impressed with how well he was handling his mother.

"No one." She pressed her lips together and sank into the chair, turning her head to stare at the wall. "Except you kids, and that won't work."

"Mom, you don't need to be here," Brooke said, but the insecurity in her eyes told Reagan otherwise. "I'll be okay."

A solution had begun to swirl in Reagan's head, but it wasn't her place to offer suggestions. Or was it? If it would help them, maybe she should speak up. Marc set Megan in his mother's arms, and Anne visibly relaxed as she held the baby.

"Marc, do you know how to make everything?" Reagan asked.

He nodded. "I do, but Rico's the only cowboy I've got at the moment. And then there's the twins. I can't leave them to head to the bakery at 4:00 a.m."

More puzzle pieces locked into place. Reagan held up her index finger. "What about this? I'll ask my sister to come out to the ranch to take care of the twins. If it's 4:00 a.m., they'll be sleeping. She'll probably bring Gemma— Gemma is her housekeeper and babysitter— with her. And you and I will go to the bakery and make all the goodies. Then you can go back to the ranch when you normally start your day, while I stay to run the bakery."

His mom opened her mouth to speak but must

have thought better of it and didn't. Marc, too, seemed to be working his way through her plan.

"Do you think Erica would be okay with it?" he asked.

"She will. She's always willing to pitch in and help in times like this."

"Sounds like it's a trait that runs in your family," Anne said. "I don't know how you dropped into our lap at just the right time, but I sure am thanking the Good Lord in my prayers for you, Reagan."

"God knew you needed some help." She gave Anne a smile. "He's sent me help when I needed it, too."

A new appreciation for her sparked in Marc's eyes, and Reagan had to look away. It was too much. The thought of him viewing her as anything beyond a temporary helper was scary. Because she wasn't doing this for him. But that look in his eyes? She'd sacrifice her time and more to see it again…and again.

How much was she willing to sacrifice for Marc Young? And was it any different from the compromises she'd made over the years, the ones she'd told herself she wasn't doing anymore?

She didn't know and didn't want to find out.

Reagan excused herself and left the room to call Erica. Her sister assured her she'd help with the twins and would ask Gemma to come with her. Gemma lived in a cabin on Erica's ranch. The woman loved children, so Reagan knew the girls would be in good hands. When she returned to the room, Brooke's eyelids were closing, and Marc's mom let out an aggressive yawn.

"The plan's on." She pocketed her phone and met Marc's gaze. "Erica will take care of the twins tomorrow."

"She knows how early she'll have to be there?" he asked.

"Yes, and she's asking Gemma to join her."

"What a relief." Anne barely got the words out before another yawn took over.

"Ma, why don't you go to your hotel room and get some rest? We need to head back to the ranch anyhow."

"I think I will." She slowly stood. "About tomorrow. I've changed the menu some. Focus on the donuts, cookies and pies. Put out a sign that we're out of everything else for the day."

"Got it," he said. "Don't worry about it another minute. I'll take care of everything."

Reagan gathered the bottles and packed everything into the diaper bag. Anne brought Megan over to Brooke to say goodbye, then buckled her into the car seat as Marc took Alice from Brooke.

"Thank you for bringing them to me today." Brooke cast a longing glance at the girls. "I'm going to work really hard this week so I can come home."

He kissed Brooke's cheek. "Don't burn yourself out. I know you'll work hard. And we'll take care of everything until you come back."

Brooke nodded, then motioned for Reagan to come over. Reagan wasn't surprised when she took her hand. His sister was beautiful, even this tired. Her almost-black hair waved around her shoulders, and she had big, round dark blue eyes, full lips and pale skin.

"Thank you," Brooke said. "Thank you from the bottom of my heart for all you're doing for my babies. I will always be in your debt."

The words brought a burst of unexpected emotion, and Reagan swallowed to ease the tightness in her throat. She patted Brooke's hand. "Like I said, I'm happy to help. You don't owe me anything."

She glanced back at Marc. Alice and Megan were secure in the stroller, and they were getting fussy. He wiped his fingers across his eyebrow as his mom listed off bakery items. Reagan pressed her lips together to keep from chuckling—why it was funny, she couldn't say—and met Brooke's eyes, also twinkling.

"She'll text him at least a hundred times about what to bake and how to bake it," Brooke said. "You'll see."

Reagan squeezed Brooke's hand once more and joined Marc. They said their goodbyes and headed down the hall.

"Was that hard for you?" She stopped at the elevators.

"Yes and no." He pressed the button. "I'm glad Brooke's improving so much, but I'm worried about her and what will happen when she and Mom come home."

"You might need help with the twins for some time." The doors opened and they went inside. Reagan smiled down at the babies. They weren't fussing anymore. They seemed to be enjoying the ride.

"I know you can't do it." Marc's shoulders slumped. "You have your own life. I'm sure we'll be able to hire some part-time help during the day."

She faltered at his words. She didn't have her own life…yet. What would *her* life look like when they didn't need her help watching the babies anymore?

It will be fine. She'd be busy with the chocolate shop. R. Mayer Chocolates would be her new life. This was just a temporary arrangement. She wouldn't forget it.

Chapter Eight

His mom would be disappointed if he messed this up. Under the dark sky, Marc fumbled with the key as he unlocked the back door of the bakery. Reagan shivered in her coat next to him. After Erica and Gemma arrived at the ranch, he'd given them the rundown on what to expect with the twins, and then he'd hopped into his truck and mentally reviewed everything his mom had texted him yesterday about the various baked items.

He couldn't remember how to make a few of the things she'd mentioned. It was a good thing she kept a binder full of her recipes at the bakery.

The lock finally clicked, and he held the door open for Reagan. As she hurried inside, he caught the tail end of the delicate floral scent of her perfume.

He switched on the lights and pointed for her to continue down the hall to the kitchen. After taking off his coat, he helped Reagan out of hers, then went to the office to hang them up. There wasn't time to catch his breath before returning to the kitchen. They had too much to do.

"Aprons are over there." He nodded at the stack in a bin under the freestanding stainless-steel workstation. Every time he was in here, the kitchen felt smaller. It could barely accommodate him and Reagan. How did his mom do this every day?

Reagan grabbed two aprons. She tossed him one, and it hit him in the chest. With her hand over her mouth, she giggled. He tried not to glare at her. It was too early for giggling, and he hadn't had even a drop of coffee yet. No one should be in a good mood this early.

"I'll put on a pot of coffee," he said.

"I'll poke around while you do."

It only took a minute to fill the carafe, scoop the grounds into the filter and get the coffee-maker started. Then he hustled next to where Reagan stood with her back to him as she reached up for something on the shelves along the wall.

Where was the recipe binder? He wasn't paying attention when she whirled around...right into his arms.

With his hands on her waist, he steadied her. "Whoa there. Where do you think you're going?"

Their bodies were close. He watched in fascination as her pupils dilated, then returned to normal. The sensation of being in her personal space made his pulse quicken. He let her go.

Today was about baking. Not Reagan.

It was impossible not to be aware of her, though—like he ever wasn't aware of her. He'd thought about her all day yesterday after they'd returned from Casper and again at night when he couldn't sleep. Her generosity, her amenable personality, her intelligence and kindness—all affected him. All tempted him.

She made him question if he *could* fit another woman into his life.

"This is great!" She rubbed her forearms. Her eyes twinkled as she took in the kitchen. "It's so cozy in here."

"Cozy is one way to put it," he said dryly. The binder. There. He opened it and set it on the counter. *Pretend she isn't here. Pretend she isn't two inches away. Pretend you can't smell her perfume.*

"What's that?" She stood all of two inches behind him and was looking over his shoulder.

How in the world was he going to pretend she wasn't there when she was practically touching him?

"Mom's recipes," he said gruffly.

"Oh, good. That will help. Or do you know how to make everything by heart?"

"Not even close." He found the page with the yeast donuts. "But Brooke and I have helped her out many times, so I'm confident we'll be able to make most of the things she sells."

"She mentioned pies. I'm not your girl for that. But cookies? Those I can handle."

He was glad she could handle cookies because, frankly, he couldn't handle being in this minuscule kitchen at all—not with her everywhere he turned. "Here's the list of what she makes on Sundays." He pulled out the laminated sheet.

Reagan took it from him as the coffeepot gurgled. He needed a cup desperately.

"Are these the quantities?" She pointed to the sheet.

"Yes. Do you want a cup?"

"Yes, please."

He poured coffee into two mugs and added cream and sugar to hers before bringing them over. She smiled her thanks, and his heart did a backflip.

Gritting his teeth, he tried to focus. *I should be checking cows. But, no, I'm in this closet of a kitchen, standing next to the most fascinating woman I've ever met, and all I can think about is touching her hair, holding her hand and learning everything there is to know about her. I need to bake.*

"What do we do first?" she asked, holding the mug between her hands.

"I'll make up the yeast dough because it needs to go into the proof box. You can work on the cookies. Then I'll get the pies started. The cake donuts don't take long. Mom's pastries are too complicated for today, but if we have time, I'll tackle a batch of bars."

"Aye, aye, Captain." With two fingers, she saluted him. The gesture was so ridiculous, he couldn't prevent the corners of his mouth from curling into a smile.

"What's that? A smile?" She grinned. "You were getting a little uptight."

"Getting? That's generous of you. I've been uptight since the minute we met."

"You have your reasons." The shrug and shimmer in her eyes made him forget why he was there.

Why was he there? *Dough. Right.* He found a mixing bowl.

"What cookies am I making first?" she asked.

He found the recipe and took it out of the binder for her. He gave her a quick overview of how to work the oven, pointed out the rack where the pans would go after baking to cool off the cookies, and then he gathered everything he needed for the donuts. They worked in silence for several minutes. Marc put the dough in the proof box to rise, started making the piecrusts and set the rounds in the fridge to chill.

Reagan popped three trays of chocolate-chip cookies into the oven and set the timer.

"Okay, Cap'n, what's next?" She glanced over her shoulder as she washed her hands at the sink.

"Sugar cookies. I'll get the recipe." He put the recipe she'd finished back in the binder and found the new one.

"You sure know your way around this place." Reagan wiped her hands off on a towel and joined him.

"Yeah, well, I had to learn." He filled the sink with soapy water and proceeded to wash the mixing bowls. "The year after my dad left, Mom and I—and Brooke, to a certain extent—worked night and day to keep our life from falling apart. If it wasn't for this bakery, we would have lost the ranch. Whenever Mom needed an extra hand or got sick, I was here to take her place."

"That's how my family is, too. We work together and pitch in when someone needs help." She dumped sugar and butter into one of the stand mixers and began creaming them together. "Yesterday, I could see how close the three of you are."

"They're my whole world." He glanced her way, and her thoughtful expression made him wonder. What did she think of him?

"It's obvious that you'd do anything for them."

"Yes." He didn't need to be reminded about why his mom was so important to him. This bakery symbolized her struggle. And a newer, bigger bakery was supposed to be her reward. But Reagan didn't know that, and he couldn't plead his case, not with all the help she'd lavished on him and the twins. And certainly not with her here helping in the bakery itself.

He cleared out the unwanted thoughts as he prepared pie fillings. Then he wiped off the counter, sprinkled flour on the workspace and took the discs of piecrust dough out of the fridge. After rolling out the crusts, he carefully transferred them to disposable pie tins, added the filling, and quickly wove the lattice top crusts. He put the pies in one of the ovens and set a timer.

"Do you have a sweet tooth?" he asked. *Duh.* Of course she did. She was opening a chocolate store.

"Oh, yeah. I'm a candyholic. Is that a word?"

"If it isn't, it should be."

"I agree. What about you?" One of the timers beeped, and Reagan took out the cookies and slid them onto the cooling rack. Then she put the next batch into the oven and meandered back to the coffeepot for another cup. When she returned, he handed her the next recipe, and she gave him another salute.

"My sweet tooth gets worse every year. I can't resist Mom's crullers. Or anything she bakes, really. She usually brings home a box of leftovers, and I go to town on them." He brushed her shoulder as he moved behind her to check the cookies on the rack. They looked perfect, from what he could tell. It didn't surprise him. Reagan's talents seemed to apply to everything she touched. "You're good at this. Do you like baking?"

"I love baking." The mixer drowned out any hope of conversation for the next couple of minutes. Reagan turned it off and continued adding ingredients.

He should be starting the next item on the list, but another cup of coffee called his name. Plus, all these questions were bubbling up. Questions he'd normally ignore but, for whatever reason, here in this small space with Reagan, he couldn't.

"Have you ever been in love?" Why had he blurted *that* out? His cheeks burned, and he hustled to the coffeemaker, where a quarter of a pot remained.

"Um, no. How about you?" She sounded nervous. He could relate.

"No."

"Really?" She looked up from where she was shaping the sugar cookie dough into a log.

"Really."

"I find that surprising." She bent down to eye level with the log and squished one end slightly. Then she straightened and took it to the refrigerator.

"I find it surprising you haven't been," he said.

After shutting the fridge's door, she wiped her hands on her apron and leaned against the counter to face him. "I haven't met the right person."

His eyebrows arched as he took a sip. "And who would that be?" Why was he asking? Why was he pursuing this at all?

"Someone who respects me. Who recognizes I have my own way of doing things. Someone who supports my decisions."

"Is that all?" His mind raced around her words and, unfortunately, came up with results he didn't like. He respected Reagan. Who wouldn't? And he had no problem with her way of doing things. But he couldn't exactly support her decision to open the chocolate shop in the corner building.

"No, it's not all. I want someone who will put

me first, the way my parents do with each other. Plus, my faith is very important to me, and I want kids."

"Yeah, I get that. Church is a big part of my life, too."

"Do you want kids?"

"If I were to ever get married, yes."

"The way you say it makes it sound like you don't plan on getting married."

"It's difficult for me to see marriage in my future."

"Why's that?"

"I've been the man of my family for fifteen years. After Brooke married Ross, I found myself alone on the ranch, and the solitude suited me. But after Ross was killed and Mom and Brooke moved back...well, it was the wake-up call I needed."

"What do you mean?"

"I'll always be here for my family. No matter what. And a wife might not understand my devotion to them. She might not support my decision to move everyone back to the ranch. But even if she did, I don't know if I could put anyone else first. My mom, my sister and the twins already have the top spot."

"I see," she said softly.

He doubted it. "I'd better get started on the cake-donut batter."

He could feel her gaze following him as he grabbed clean mixing bowls. Reagan wanted someone who would put her first. She deserved it. Part of him wished he could be that guy.

Marc scooped flour into one of the bowls. His life was a raging mess at the moment. The one thing he didn't need was romance, and he wasn't going to go looking for it. He'd push away these inconvenient feelings. He had enough on his mind to last a century anyhow.

Reagan was tired all the way to her bones. In five minutes, she could flip the Open sign to Closed and lock the bakery…if she didn't pass out from exhaustion first.

She took a spray bottle and clean cloth over to the three café tables and wiped them down. Then she cleaned the chairs and put away the supplies. The bakery was open from seven in the morning until two in the afternoon. Add the hours of baking earlier and it had been the longest ten hours of her life.

It wasn't that she hadn't enjoyed it. She had. Making all the baked goods with Marc this morning had been fun, informative—even flirty. Every day she learned something new about him. All the tidbits were adding up to give her a better picture of who he was. When he'd left before the bakery opened to relieve

Rico from cattle duty, Reagan had immediately missed him.

Everyone who'd come in to the bakery had been welcoming. She'd spent hour after hour filling bags and boxes with donuts and pies and everything else. The register hadn't been too complicated, and what she didn't know, the customers had been eager to explain. It had been really nice to get to know the residents of Jewel River better.

The only thing she was confused about had nothing to do with Marc or baking or customers. It had happened earlier, when she'd toured the bakery. It had been so sudden and unexpected that she still hadn't processed it.

When she'd walked through the space, she'd instantly pictured the interior of Annie's Bakery, from the front to the rear, completely reconfigured to be her chocolate shop.

As it was, the bakery was functional and cozy and smelled delicious. But somehow, in a flash, she'd mentally reconfigured the layout, redecorated it and replaced the current bakery display with her chocolate display cases. The front wall? Gone. It would be replaced with large windows and a glass door to let in light. Those three café tables? No room—and no need—for them.

The vision of her chocolate shop still blazed

in her mind. And she didn't know what to do with it.

Reagan checked the time and decided to lock up a few minutes early. If even one more customer came in, she'd collapse in a heap on the floor and start whimpering. She was just that tired.

She was almost to the door when it opened. *No way. I'm telling them we're closed. I can't fake a smile right now. I can't. I just can't.*

But to her surprise, Erica and Gemma entered the store.

"Quick, flip over the sign!" Reagan pointed to the door. "Before anyone else comes in."

Erica's eyes grew round, but she backtracked and flipped the sign. "Want me to lock the door?"

"Yes." She resumed her spot behind the counter, took out two large donut boxes and began filling them with the few leftovers that hadn't sold. "You're taking these home with you."

"But Gemma already made me snickerdoodles."

"That's true. I did, dear." Gemma pulled out a chair and groaned.

"Are you okay, Gemma?" Reagan asked.

"Just a little tired. Johnny's coming over later. He might like the donuts."

"See?" Reagan beamed to Erica. "Johnny will like the donuts."

"Those babies are delightful," Gemma said. "But it's been ages since I've been up this early to care for infants."

"Me, too." Erica collapsed onto the chair opposite Gemma.

"Why are you here so early? Who's watching the twins?" Reagan finished filling the boxes. Then she wrinkled her nose at the register. "I have no idea what Anne does with the money."

"Is there a cash bag?" Erica asked.

Reagan rummaged through the drawer and cabinet below the register. She found a pouch of some sort and held it up. "Is this it?"

"Yes. Just put the cash and receipts in there. Do you need help cleaning the kitchen?"

"No, Marc and I took care of it before I opened the store this morning. I'll just give the floors a quick mop, and I'll be done. You still haven't told me who is watching the girls."

"Oh, right. Anne came home half an hour ago. She said the move went well, and that Brooke was already working on her mobility assignments when she left."

"That's good news. I'm glad she came home early. This is the first time she's been home in almost a week."

"Maybe we should have stayed so Anne could take a nap." Gemma frowned, biting her lower lip.

"We tried," Erica said to Gemma. "She wouldn't hear of it."

"You're right, but still."

Reagan filled the mop bucket and almost broke her back trying to get it out of the deep sink in the utility closet. Using the mop handle, she steered the bucket on wheels to the front of the store and began to mop. "Thank you both for going over there so early and helping out with the babies. I really appreciate it."

"We were happy to, weren't we?" Erica said, smiling at Gemma.

"Yes, but maybe a little later in the morning next time."

All three of them laughed. Reagan's back and shoulders ached as she mopped her way to the rear of the store and into the kitchen. With Anne home in the afternoons, Reagan probably wouldn't have to coordinate babysitters for the twins anymore.

She dumped out the dirty water and put the supplies back in the utility closet. After washing her hands, she found her coat and purse and joined Erica and Gemma.

"I'm not sure what's going to happen next week with the twins." Reagan motioned for them to follow her to the back door. They emerged outside moments later. "Anne said she's going to be home in the afternoons, so I'm assuming

Marc won't be driving to Casper anymore. If I watch the babies until Anne comes home, the two of them will probably be able to take care of Megan and Alice on their own."

Erica put her arm around Reagan's shoulders. "If you want to take off time to work on the business, we'll find babysitters to come out in the mornings."

The gesture and thought behind it were kind, but Reagan bristled anyway.

"That's okay. Ed's getting an estimate to me this coming week. I've got everything under control."

"But I know you want to paint your house and—"

"It doesn't need to get done right now."

"But—"

"It can wait."

Erica's gaze probed her for a long moment. Then she glanced around. "Where's your car?"

"Marc picked me up."

"Want a ride home?"

Normally, she'd decline. She loved fresh air, especially after being indoors most of the winter. But if she didn't get off her feet soon, she didn't know what would happen.

"I'd love a ride home."

Five minutes later, she waved goodbye to them and let herself into her house. She put on her softest joggers and favorite old sweatshirt with a big stain on the sleeve. Then she padded to the couch, stretched out her legs and closed her eyes.

Every muscle twitched. Every joint ached. And every thought ping-ponged between her vision of the chocolate shop being in the bakery and her interaction with Marc this morning.

He'd asked some personal questions. Given her personal answers. What he'd told her yesterday about his father leaving and then him taking over the ranch had become more nuanced today when he'd talked about his mom and the bakery. Anne's sacrifices had clearly touched him deeply. Reagan understood why he was invested in her success. She also understood why he'd moved his sister and the twins in with him. And she got his worries about finding a woman who not only grasped why he did the things he did for his family, but also approved of them.

But he didn't seem to think he was capable of putting a wife's needs up there with his mom's and sister's. And if he wasn't, there was no future for Reagan to be with him. She wasn't willing to settle for anything less than his top spot.

"I can't move." Marc lengthened the recliner as far as it would go. Megan was asleep in his arms. His mom was stretched out on the couch with her head on a pillow from her bedroom. Alice was sleeping on her chest. Earlier, he and his mom had warmed up a can of tomato soup and choked down a few grilled cheese sandwiches. It was all either of them had had the energy to make or to eat.

Had it only been this morning when he'd met Reagan at the bakery? Felt like a thousand years ago.

The television was turned to a cooking show that neither of them was watching. The noise from it relaxed him, though.

"Longest week of your life?" he asked, keeping his head against the headrest.

"By far. You?"

"Oh, yeah."

"I haven't even asked how the cattle are doing."

"They're good. Tagged another calf this morning."

"Glad to hear it."

The television was the only sound in the room for quite a while.

"What are we going to do until Brooke comes home? You know, about the twins and the bakery?" Marc asked. He didn't want to think about it, but they had to come up with a plan. Last week was a blur of Reagan arriving, him checking cattle, driving to the hospital, coming home to awkward conversations with the volunteers, then forcing himself to eat before crashing in bed. Reagan had already told him she'd be at the ranch tomorrow morning, but they couldn't sustain this for long. She'd already done so much for them.

"I can't think about it now," she said.

"Fair enough."

He wanted to close his eyes and sleep for days, but his practical side won out. He snapped the recliner back to normal and stood, regretting it as his knees and hips cried out, then carried Megan upstairs and gently placed her in her crib. He returned to the living room and took Alice from his mother, then went back upstairs and put her to bed, too.

After changing into sweatpants and a T-shirt, he brushed his teeth and reclaimed his spot on the recliner. Mom was conked out, her mouth ajar as she lightly snored. For the first time, it hit him that she looked old. Not senior-citizen old, just every inch of her fifty-nine years. It was no wonder after the week they'd had.

He drew the comforter over her, then took his spot on the recliner once more.

Marc had reached a breaking point today. It was all too much. He'd called Cade and Ty and Dalton about hiring another cowboy to get through calving. Ty had gotten back to him a few hours ago. One of his ranch hands had a brother who'd been helping them part-time and was looking for more work. Ty vouched for Trevor's experience and said he had good instincts with the cattle. Trevor would be at Marc's ranch tomorrow morning.

He should have hired someone earlier in the season. He'd foolishly told himself he and Rico would be fine dealing with calving on their own. But he'd been wrong. If Trevor worked out, he and Rico could get some much-needed rest.

And, no matter what way he sliced it, it was obvious his mother needed another part-time employee, too. Sure, she and Deb managed the bakery fine in normal times, but the second the twins had been born, everything had stopped being normal.

That led to the next issue. The twins. It was wishful thinking to imagine Brooke would be able to care for them on her own when she was released from the hospital. And he and Mom were spread too thin as it was. They needed to hire part-time help until Brooke recovered completely. But how would his sister feel about it?

Reagan had offered time and again to babysit until Brooke came home. Why couldn't he simply accept her help? She was great with the twins. Sure, he hated the feeling of being in her debt, but he didn't know how they would have survived without her help.

God, I haven't taken enough time to pray beyond asking You to heal my sister. But thank You for sending Reagan. We needed her. We still need her. I know we're taking advantage of her generosity, but I can barely deal with everything as it is. And knowing the twins are in her capable hands gives me the breathing room I need.

Their conversation while baking this morning came back to him. She was easy to talk to. He'd told her things he hadn't told anyone. He usually didn't discuss how hard it had been for his mom to get the bakery running or how overwhelmed he'd been when he'd single-handedly taken over the ranch. And he never talked about his romantic life. Maybe because he didn't have a romantic life. The last time he'd dated anyone had been three or four years ago. A teacher at the elementary school. Nice woman. Phoebe was now married with a baby on the way.

He had no regrets.

He would have only disappointed Phoebe, and she would have left him for someone who could meet her needs. So, he'd broken things off. But Reagan… She was unique. She not only understood how much his mom, sister and nieces meant to him, but she threw herself wholeheartedly into helping them, too.

What did he have to offer a woman like her? He didn't even know what she needed.

That's not true. She told you.

He closed his eyes, replaying her melodic voice in the bakery this morning. She wanted someone who respected her.

Who wouldn't respect her? She was something special.

She'd also mentioned that she had her own way of doing things, and if he remembered correctly from previous conversations, her family didn't think her way was the right way. Hadn't she said she second-guessed herself a lot?

Then the clincher—she needed a man who would support her decisions and who would put her first.

Marc's heart sank. He lived with strong women. He supported their decisions, even when he didn't like them. But he didn't know if he could put a girlfriend or a wife first. When all this was said and done, he'd find a way to thank Reagan, and he'd resume his solitary life.

Chapter Nine

Reagan's palms grew clammy as she kept an eye on the library entrance Thursday afternoon. *What if this is a mistake? What if he thinks I'm an idiot? What if he treats me like I'm incompetent?*

She'd found an empty table near the teen section. Her laptop, notebook, pen and phone were lined up in front of her. If Slim Nixon thought she was an idiot, she'd handle it. Somehow. *Yeah, like you handled it when Mom acted like you'd requested a unicorn for your birthday when you told her you were going to Denver?*

The only reason she hadn't caved to her mother's pressure to stay in Sunrise Bend was that she'd already lined up the chocolate job and put a deposit down on a short-term furnished rental. Reagan knew herself too well. One sign of doubt from her family and she'd fold like a cheap lounge chair.

If Slim gave her the impression he thought she

was in over her head, she'd just have to thank him and excuse herself. She'd drive straight to Erica's and beg her for help. Trying to figure out all these business forms was over her head by a mile, and she was tired of pretending otherwise.

A tall gentleman with a silver mustache and wearing a navy vest over a button-down shirt, jeans and cowboy boots walked through the doors. Rising slightly, she waved, and he acknowledged her with a nod.

"Reagan Mayer, I assume?" He leaned across the table and held out his hand. "It's good to meet you."

"Thanks for agreeing to come here. I'm… well…" She was getting flustered, and it had nothing to do with Slim. She just felt so out of her league.

"You don't have to say a word. I understand. It's a lot to figure out." He took a seat and opened a folder. "Clem mentioned a chocolate shop."

She nodded, unsure of what to say or what to do.

"Good, good. I like chocolates. Especially chocolate-covered strawberries. Do you make those?"

"I do." If Slim could help her wade through all this, she'd make him a dozen chocolate-covered strawberries every week for the rest of his life.

"I'll be stopping in for them once your shop is

open." His friendly tone set her at ease. "Now, why don't you tell me where you're at in the process?"

She swallowed, trying to tamp down her nerves. "Not very far."

"Have you picked out a name for your business?" He clicked open a pen.

"Yes. R. Mayer Chocolates."

"Good, good." He jotted it down. "And how do you want to structure the company?"

"Structure?" The word brought to mind steel beams and concrete, but she doubted that was what he'd meant.

"You can incorporate or create a limited liability company." He explained the different types of businesses and their pros and cons.

Right. Now she understood what he meant by structure. After going back and forth about the options, both agreed on which one would make the most sense for her.

"Okay," Slim said, "let's pull up the Wyoming Secretary of State website and do a search to make sure your company name isn't taken already. Then we can register it."

"Right now?"

"Sure. Why not?"

It was as if the dark clouds surrounding her to-do list had parted. What a blessing this man was. Slim wasn't just telling her what she needed to do—he was helping her do it.

Over the next hour, they were able to submit three forms to various agencies. He gave her instructions to work on the others at home. When they finished, he escorted her out the door to her car.

"Now, if you have any questions—I don't care how small they might seem—you give me a call." He shook her hand once more.

"Wait. How much do I owe you?" She should have asked before they'd gotten started, but whatever price he threw out, she'd happily pay him.

"I'll take a couple of those chocolate-covered strawberries after your shop opens."

"But I can't let you do all this work without paying you. I want to—"

"Nope. I'm retired. I like helping folks out. And you seem like an awful nice person to help."

She blinked as her emotions got the better of her. What a kind, generous man. "The next time I see you, expect to take home a box of those chocolate-covered strawberries."

"I'm looking forward to it."

They parted, and Reagan got into her car and swiped her phone. She almost pressed Marc's number. But then she remembered that this conversation was off-limits with him. By his choice.

She sighed. It was too bad, really. They got along so well. Every morning when she arrived at the ranch, they had a cup of coffee together and discussed Brooke and the bakery and the calves. While he didn't seem to mind talking about making the chocolate—he hadn't showed any discomfort Tuesday when she'd mentioned all the equipment she'd ordered—he *did* mind any mention of the building. The few times she'd broached the subject, his jaw had tightened and the light in his eyes had gone out.

So she'd kept it to herself when Ed McCaffrey had called her yesterday to let her know he'd have the estimate ready this Friday. And she hadn't mentioned this meeting with Slim, either.

It seemed their relationship only worked on his terms. And that wasn't much of a relationship at all. If she couldn't share the things most important to her, then maybe she'd be better off not putting too much stock in their friendship.

After starting her vehicle, she drove down Center Street. She flicked a glance at the bakery. What was it about that particular space that appealed to her so? It was a hidden gem, for sure. Continuing on, she parked in front of her building. Without getting out of the car, she stared at the entrance, and all the anticipation she expected to feel was nowhere to be found.

What was her problem? Why wasn't it singing to her the way the bakery just had? Was she letting Marc's attitude about it get to her? Was she internalizing his disapproval and getting cold feet because of it? Trying to find a compromise so he'd let her into his world?

Pulling her shoulders back, she checked her rearview and backed out of the spot. Her chocolate shop would be in *this* building. The plans were moving forward. She'd made a lot of progress this week with the help of Ed and now Slim. It would be ridiculous to let Marc's bias affect her decisions.

This was her life, not his, and she was making the best of it. Starting with this building. If he didn't like it, too bad.

But as she approached the intersection to turn left, she couldn't help but wish he'd get on board. The building—her plans for it—was the only thing that seemed to be standing between them. And she'd spent enough time with him over the past couple of weeks to know she liked him. A lot. But if he couldn't respect her decisions...

She'd better put some ice on that attraction. She had too much to lose if she didn't.

"I don't know about that." Marc set his mug on the counter Friday morning as he kept a firm grip on Alice. He was just starting to feel like himself again—a tired version of himself—and now Reagan was asking him to do this?

The week had gone better than he'd hoped. Brooke was making excellent progress, and the doctors were already talking about letting her come home later next week. Mom had been visiting her every other day and working at the bakery on the days she stayed in town. Trevor, the ranch hand Ty had recommended, was a hard worker who needed little supervision. Hiring the cowboy had allowed both Marc and Rico to catch up on lost sleep.

"Do you have something against taking pictures of the girls around the ranch?" Reagan held Megan in her left arm and calmly sipped her coffee. "It's a beautiful day, and I think Brooke would really appreciate seeing them in cute outfits outdoors."

"Why the ranch?"

She lifted one shoulder in a shrug. "I've taken pictures of them on their play mat and in their bouncy seats. Why not get them in the sunshine?" She set the mug down to snap her fingers. "What about taking their picture with one of the calves? You have a few in the corrals, don't you?"

"Ye-e-es." He grabbed his coffee again and took another drink. "Is it safe for the girls to be around livestock?"

"I don't know. I just thought it would be fun to have one in the picture."

"I suppose."

"When these two get older, they're going to love the calves. You can't stop my nieces and nephews from petting them. Clara and Maddie kiss them on the forehead. It's really cute."

"I don't want these two kissing any cows."

Her laughter loosened the tension spreading across his upper back. "I don't think we need to worry about them kissing cows just yet. I saw the most adorable little sundresses and headbands in their closet. Would it be okay for me to dress them up?"

How would he know? His sister's plans for their clothes had gone out the door when she had the stroke.

"If it's not, I'll just find different outfits," she said. "But it sure would be cute to have them in those dresses."

"Go ahead," he said. "If Brooke or Mom say anything, I'll take the blame."

"Do you think they would?" Worry lines creased her forehead.

"No, not really." All week his mom had raved about Reagan every time her name was mentioned. And it was mentioned often. Too often. "Knowing those two, they'll probably love it."

"Good. And, listen, if you don't want the girls

near a calf, that's fine. There are so many places on your ranch that will make a good photo op."

Photo op? It was news to him. While he loved his property, he was under no illusions. Anywhere you walked, you were going to smell manure. He kept the grounds tidy and the fences repaired, but it wasn't anyone's dream spot for selfies and photo shoots.

"I'm thinking I'll bring out that adorable quilt with the pastel colors I saw in the closet. And correct me if I'm wrong, but I did see kittens running around near the stables, didn't I?"

"You did. But I don't see how we can get barn kittens to cooperate with getting their picture taken."

"Point taken." Her face glowed with excitement. It made him want to say yes to everything she suggested. "No problem. We'll get plenty of other shots with the girls."

Her enthusiasm lifted his spirits. Reagan was right. This break in the weather was too good to pass up. The girls had never experienced being outside without being bundled up. And even then they'd simply been transferred from the house to the minivan. Fresh air and sunshine would do them both some good.

"What time do you want to take the girls out?" he asked.

"Let's do it after lunch. They'll be fresh from

their nap. I know it means taking an hour out of your day, so if you have to check cattle or whatever, I understand. I just don't think I can get the pictures I want without your help."

He hiked Alice farther up his shoulder. "I can take an hour off. It's okay."

She nodded, a twinge of insecurity in her expression. He didn't like that she felt insecure about asking him for this. The twins were important to him.

"It'll be time well spent," he said. "Brooke is going to love it, and it will probably motivate her to work even harder so she can come home."

"I really hope the doctors clear her to move back soon." Reagan shifted Megan, kissing the top of her head in the process.

"Me, too." Disappointment settled in his gut. He figured Reagan was probably itching to get back to her own life. "Listen, we appreciate your sacrifice in coming out here every day. If you have stuff you need to do, just let me know. We can line up another babysitter or something. I know you have a lot to take care of."

"What? Oh, no, that's not why I said it. I want her to move home so she can be with her babies and start getting back to normal. I can't imagine how awful it would be to be separated from the twins for so long."

Of course. He should have known she would

think of Brooke's feelings over her own inconvenience. This had nothing to do with her wanting her own life back. Why had he automatically gone there?

"Yeah, I want it for her, too." He drank the last of his coffee and set the mug in the sink. Then he lifted Alice up in the air near his face. "And you, little princess, be good for Reagan this morning. You and your sister are going to get a tour of the ranch after lunch. If you're good, you can see a calf. Maybe even some kittens." He kissed her nose and met Reagan's eyes. They sparkled with mirth and something else... Appreciation.

It was nice to feel appreciated.

"Where should I put her?" he asked.

"Let's try the play mat first. The girls can have some wiggle time down there."

"You got it." As he made his way to the living room, he wanted to ask her how her plans were coming along for the chocolate shop. The other day she'd told him about all the things she'd ordered—a machine to temper the chocolate, double boilers, food scales and all kinds of things he hadn't realized she would need—and he'd liked listening to her. Wanted to know more about her plans. But instead of asking the questions her list had brought up, a hard ball had formed in his chest and the words wouldn't come out.

Instead, he'd recalled all the times his mom had talked about moving the bakery to the corner building. She'd described exactly how she would display the baked goods in the windows for the holidays. And her eyes had sparkled as she'd estimated all the additional seating she'd have and how more people could hang out there in the mornings.

His mom had all these dreams, all these plans. And they all revolved around the place Reagan was using for her dreams, her plans.

Marc never thought he'd be in a dilemma about wanting to support his mom while at the same time rooting for the woman who stood in the way of his mother's dream coming true.

But this was Reagan. No ordinary woman. Didn't she deserve to have her dreams come true, too?

He carefully set Alice on the mat. A few seconds later, Reagan placed Megan next to her. When she straightened, he didn't step back, leaving them only inches apart. Attraction flared. He wanted to say something, do something, but the moment passed.

"I'll be back after lunch for the pictures." He didn't bother waiting for her reply, just hurried out of the room with his face hotter than a broiler. *Come on, Marc, you're thirty-two. Grow up.*

This feeling had nothing to do with maturity, though. He was falling for Reagan Mayer, and it terrified him.

"It's perfect!" Reagan couldn't believe Marc had come up with this. He'd found an oval galvanized tub and lined it with the quilt she'd mentioned earlier. The tub was nestled in the grass near a fence with hay bales stacked next to it. "Are you sure you weren't a photographer's assistant at some point?"

"I'm sure." He grinned, adjusting the quilt.

"And you didn't help design sets for the school plays?" She liked teasing him. The twitch of his lips and creases in the corners of his eyes told her he enjoyed it, too.

"Afraid not."

"Well, you got your talent somewhere."

"Probably my mom." He chuckled.

"Probably." Reagan knelt and laid Alice on the quilt in the tub, then held out her hands for Marc to pass Megan to her. He did, and she settled the girls next to each other. Then she straightened their little sundresses and headbands and stood. They stared up at her with wide-eyed expressions.

"Okay, you stay close to them, and I'll take the

pictures." She slid her phone from her pocket. Then she moved around to get the best angles. She took close-ups and pictures from above and from the side. When she was satisfied she'd gotten enough pictures, she faced Marc and held up her phone. "These turned out perfect."

"Let me see."

She handed it to him and watched as he swiped through them. "I still want to get a picture of them with a calf."

Chuckling, he picked up Megan, cradling her to one shoulder, then picked up Alice. He made carrying two babies look easy. And Reagan knew from experience it was tricky. She gathered the quilt, folded it and shoved it in the basket under the stroller. "Do you want the girls in here?"

"Nah, I'll carry them." He smiled at Megan, then Alice. "You like being out here, don't you? Just wait until summer. You're going to love it even more."

Reagan pushed the stroller as they headed toward the barns.

"I moved one of the calves to a pen earlier so you can get some pictures."

They continued past the barn to the corrals and a pen behind it. A little calf had curled up on the grass next to the fencing, and a gray kitten was sleeping against its side.

"Marc, would you look at that?" She pointed to the calf with the kitten. "How precious. I have to get a picture."

She entered the pen and quickly got a few shots of the sleeping calf with the kitten. Then she stepped back. "Hmm…any ideas on how to get a picture with the girls?"

"Why don't you crouch down there with them, and I'll take the picture?"

"I think Brooke would prefer to see you with them. You're their uncle."

"Yeah, but you're prettier."

He thought she was pretty? She liked the sound of that.

They argued back and forth about who should be in the photo, until finally Marc relented. Reagan helped him hold the girls so they would be cradled in each of his arms and facing the camera. Then he crouched on one knee next to the calf. Reagan started taking pictures. The kitten yawned, stretched her front legs and settled more deeply into sleep. The calf woke and looked up at Marc.

"Hey there, little guy," Marc said as the calf licked his arm. He shifted so the girls could see it. "You've got a couple of friends here today."

The calf extended his neck to sniff Megan. The babies couldn't take their eyes off him. Megan reached out and touched its soft forehead.

Reagan took picture after picture, knowing she was going to love each one more than the previous. After a few minutes, Marc winced.

"Would you take Alice for me? I'm in an awkward position, and I don't trust myself not to stumble getting up."

"No problem." She put away her phone and took the baby.

"What next?" He rose, holding Megan, and opened the gate for them. She gave the calf one more smile and exited the pen.

"It's so nice out. I don't want to go back inside yet. I think I'll spread out the quilt on the lawn for a bit."

"I'll join you." They strapped the girls into the stroller, and Marc pushed it in the direction of his backyard.

"Tell me about this place." She glanced around the outbuildings and took in the pastures.

"The ranch?"

"Yeah."

"My grandparents—my mother's folks— were newlyweds when they bought it. The farmhouse was already here and most of the outbuildings were, too. Mom grew up on the ranch. My grandfather died shortly after my parents married. Mom and Dad talked with my grandmother, and they agreed to take over the ranch for her. They moved into the farmhouse, and my grandmother moved to an apartment in town."

"That's sad about your grandfather, but I love that it worked out so your parents could take over." She pointed to a dry grassy area. "Is this okay?"

"Sure." He stopped the stroller, took the quilt out and spread it on the grass. They each took a baby and sat on the quilt. "Anyway, my grandmother passed away not long after I turned sixteen. It was hard. Brooke and I were really close to her. Being an only child, Mom inherited the ranch, along with all of my grandmother's assets. My parents argued about the inheritance. Then my father left us. A week after my grandmother's funeral."

As the impact of what he was saying hit her, Reagan tried not to cringe. His father leaving them had been awful, but the circumstances made it even worse. Leaving so soon after his wife's mother died?

"I'm so sorry. I don't know what to say."

"There's nothing to say. From a young age, I worked alongside my father and our full-time cowboy on this land. And the second Mom inherited it, Dad walked away, knowing he'd get half of everything in the divorce. It was like this ranch meant nothing to him."

The unspoken words unraveled between

them—Reagan could practically hear him say, *Like we meant nothing to him.*

"Didn't he like ranching?" she asked and immediately regretted it. She shouldn't be prying into such a sore subject.

"I thought he liked it. I mean, I never suspected he didn't." He stared off into the distance. "All of Grandma's money was used to pay off my dad. We had to sell acreage, too. And he took it. Took everything and left."

Reagan wanted to comfort him but, in this moment, she had no idea how. "Why? Why would he do that?"

"I don't know. I've asked myself that question too many times." He shifted to face her. The pain in his eyes broke her heart. "Why would he take everything that mattered to us? Why did he leave?"

Alice began to squirm and, as if on cue, Megan got fussy.

"They're ready for a nap. I should get them back inside." Reagan moved to a kneeling position before standing. She held Alice close and caressed her little cheek. Then she settled her back in the stroller. Marc buckled Megan in the stroller, too, and folded the quilt.

"I'll help you get them inside."

She pushed the stroller, steadying it as it hit a rut, with Marc next to her. As soon as they reached the side porch, Marc unbuckled the babies, both on the verge of crying, and carried them inside. "Just leave all that out here. I'll take care of it later."

Reagan went straight to the kitchen, washed her hands and went to the fridge to pull out the bottles she'd prepared earlier. She placed them in the bottle warmer.

"Should I change them out of these dresses?" Marc called from the living room.

"Yes, please." She filled a glass of water as the thump of his footsteps up the staircase echoed. Having him help right now was a relief. Her energy always flagged in the afternoon, and her upper back muscles and arms tended to ache from carrying the twins. From upstairs, the twins' cries reached her. Neither of them wanted to get their diapers and clothes changed, apparently.

Several minutes later, Marc descended the stairs with the babies—in onesies and stretchy pants—in his arms. Both girls continued to cry. Reagan rushed over, took Megan and gently bounced her on the way to the couch. The bottles were on the end table. She held one to Megan's mouth, but she was crying hard, and it took her a few tries before she'd take the bottle.

Marc had already given Alice hers and was

sitting in the recliner. As soon as the crying halted, a sense of peace filled the air.

"Reagan?" he asked.

"Yeah?"

"Thanks for listening." His face was drawn. "I feel comfortable talking to you. Comfortable being with you."

The compliment spilled down to her toes, and she gave him a smile. "You're welcome."

"When life is back to normal, I hope…well… I hope we'll still be friends."

"I hope so, too." It was on the tip of her tongue to say *Of course we'll still be friends— why wouldn't we be?* but she couldn't in good faith say it. Because when he no longer needed help with the twins, they'd have no reason to hang out. And when the work on her building started, Marc wouldn't want to spend time with her anyhow.

With that in mind, she decided to tell it to him straight. No more keeping her plans to herself to protect his feelings. "I'm expecting the estimate for renovating my building from Ed Mc-Caffrey this afternoon."

"Oh." Was she imagining the regret in his tone? "He's a good contractor. He'll take care of you."

His response was more than she'd expected. Yet it was less than what she'd hoped for.

"I suppose this means you'll be ready to file for permits soon."

"I suppose it does."

When he didn't say anything, she tried to bury her disappointment. She'd always been one to take things to heart. Just like she'd also always been one to see the writing on the wall.

Marc had made it abundantly clear where his priorities were. And she'd never be one of them.

She doubted friendship would ever be enough for her, and anything more was off the table from his point of view. If she kept reminding herself she couldn't have him, maybe she'd be able to convince herself she didn't want him.

Or was it already too late?

She didn't know and didn't want to find out.

Chapter Ten

The following Thursday, Marc helped Brooke out of the passenger seat of the minivan. Her shining eyes filled with tears as she gave him a grateful smile. He hadn't seen her smile like that since before Ross died. A dart of hope pierced his heart.

"It feels like I haven't been here in years." She threw both of her arms around him and hugged him tightly. Her left arm put the same pressure on him as her right. She really had made a lot of progress.

She still had a limp, but it wasn't as noticeable as it had been when she'd first arrived at the rehab center. It was astounding how much she'd healed in less than two weeks.

Mom got out of the back seat and went straight to the trunk to grab Brooke's belongings. Hauling two large bags, she marched past them, then gestured with her head to the minivan. "There are a few more bags back there, Marc."

"Got it." He squeezed Brooke's hand and she squeezed it back. "Let me help Brooke inside first."

He tucked her arm in his, and they slowly made their way up the porch steps and into the mudroom.

"Are you doing okay?" he asked.

"Better than okay. I'm nervous about the stairs, but I think I could have managed the porch steps fine without your help." Brooke paused to get her bearings near the doorway to the kitchen. "Before we go in there, I just want to thank you. For everything. Moving me back here after Ross died. Helping with the twins before I had the stroke. Taking care of them after the stroke. I couldn't ask for a better brother. All of this must have been exhausting for you. On top of that, I know I haven't been easy to be around for a long time."

Marc gave her another hug. "I wanted to be here for you. You went through a lot after Ross died. We didn't expect you to be floating on happy clouds all the time."

"Thanks." She placed her hand on his arm and inhaled deeply. "I'm ready for my babies. I'm going in."

"You need my help?" He wasn't sure if he should insist on walking her into the living room, where Reagan had the girls, or let her do it on her own.

She shook her head. "No. I've been working hard. I can handle this."

"I'll get those other bags."

A few minutes later, he entered the living room as his mother fussed with pillows for Brooke, who was sitting on the couch. Brooke held Alice and was raving about how much the girls had grown in her absence, while Reagan knelt on the play mat and dangled a stuffed elephant above Megan. He'd been prepared for awkward silence, but it wasn't the case. In three seconds flat, the women had found a conversational rhythm he'd never understand.

"I think we should set up a bed in the dining room for you, honey. That way you don't have to worry about the stairs." His mom gave a pillow one final pat, then straightened and frowned as she looked around for something.

"Too much work. I don't plan on using the stairs unless I'm going to bed or showering." Brooke's tone was pleasant as she made silly faces for Alice. "Everything I need for the day is down here. I want my routine back."

"We could move more of the girls' clothes down here for you." Reagan shifted to sit cross-legged next to Megan. "That way, if they need a complete outfit change, you wouldn't have to worry."

He caught his mother's frown as she left the room.

"That's a good idea," Brooke said. "And more diapers, more wipes. They nap in their portable cribs."

Was Brooke being too optimistic? Maybe Mom was right that Brooke should move down here until she...what? He didn't know. Wasn't sure if the limp would go away or not. But one thing he did know? Trying to take care of two babies was going to be difficult with or without the stairs.

His mother rushed back with her arms full of bedding. She dropped a folded blanket and a comforter on the couch. "You can nap here until we figure out the sleeping situation."

His mom's I-know-what's-best tone alerted him to trouble. Marc slowly inched back toward the kitchen. He wanted no part of this upcoming conversation.

Brooke glanced at Mom. "My physical therapist told me I should push myself to do everything I did before the stroke, and when I get tired, to listen to my body and rest."

"I know." His mom pursed her lips, clearly

keeping her frustration in check. "But you're not ready for stairs."

"Doctor Cleese told me I was." Brooke brought Alice up to her shoulder, sat back and addressed her mother. "I know I'm not all the way there yet, especially with my left leg. But I worked really hard—hours every day—to come here and have my life back. Can't we at least try it my way for a week?"

Marc was surprised at how calm Brooke sounded.

"And what exactly is your way?" Mom asked.

"If we hire someone to come in and help with the babies until you get home from the bakery, I won't worry about not being able to handle the girls. Plus, it will free up some time for me to continue with my exercises."

"I think we need to do that no matter what." His mom took a seat in one of the chairs. "But even with the help, you going up and down the stairs makes me nervous…"

As the back-and-forth continued, he made his way through the living room to crouch near Reagan.

"Hey," he said gently.

"Hey." Her eyes twinkled.

"Thanks for being here," he said so only she could hear. "This morning went smoothly.

Knowing the twins were in good hands helped a lot."

"I love watching them." She kept her voice low as she glanced at Megan with eyes full of affection. The baby was mouthing a toy.

Brooke's voice grew louder. "If you or Marc help me, I can get up those stairs at night and down them again in the morning."

"What if you need something in the night?" Mom was starting to get snippy.

His sister huffed. "I'll wake one of you up."

"You promise? I know how you are. Never wanting anyone to help. Not wanting to be a burden. This is important, Brooke."

He exchanged a charged look with Reagan. Then he held out his hand. She took it, and he helped her to her feet. "Come on. Let's get out of here for a little while."

"Are you sure?"

"Where are you going?" his mother demanded.

"We're getting some fresh air." He took a few steps, then turned back. "Why don't you both just relax and enjoy this for the moment? We'll get everything sorted out later."

Mom closed her mouth, shaking her head, and Brooke mouthed *Thank you* to him.

He hitched his chin to her and led Reagan through the kitchen to the mudroom. After she put on her shoes, they went outside. The sun was shining and a light breeze blew.

"She seems to be doing well." Reagan strolled next to him on their way to the outbuildings.

"Yeah. It's more than physical, too. There's a new spark to her that was missing before the stroke."

"What do you mean?"

"I don't know. I feel like ever since Ross died, she's been barely holding on to get through life. Mom and I were worried about her. But today? It's like having my sister back—all of her."

They continued in easy silence until they reached the fence to the horse pasture. The horses were loving this warmer weather, too. Their tails flicked as they grazed.

With one arm resting on a fence post, he turned to Reagan. He didn't know if it was the relief of having Brooke home, the realization that the worst month of his life was almost over or his growing feelings for the quiet beauty by his side, but he couldn't keep his thoughts inside anymore.

"Reagan, I couldn't have gotten through this without you."

Wind tickled the tendrils of hair around her face as she turned to him. But she didn't speak. Now that he had her alone, the thoughts he'd been avoiding all came to a head.

"I don't want this—what we have—to end."

"What do we have, Marc?" She sounded curious, not sarcastic.

"I'm not sure. I just know I like being with you and want to spend more time with you."

"As friends?"

"Yes. And more." He shrugged, staring at the horses again. Had he really admitted that? Was he ready for more?

Would he ever be ready?

"I like being with you, too." She averted her eyes.

"But?"

"But I don't think we can get close enough for more."

The words surprised him. Why would she think that?

"Why not?"

She gave him a deadpan look. "There seem to be topics that are off-limits between us."

"That's not true."

"It is true." Her probing stare made him flinch. "I can't talk to you about my plans for the building."

He couldn't refute it but... "I liked hearing about all the supplies you ordered."

"I'll give you that," she said. "But whenever I mention the building, your face gets all pinched, and I can feel the strain between us."

Okay, it was true. He wasn't sure how he could overcome it, though.

"On Tuesday, Ed and I went over the plans and estimates for the building, and I hired him for the job. He's already filed for the building permit. I wanted to tell you all this yesterday, but I didn't feel like I could. So I kept it to myself."

He hadn't realized… Wasn't really prepared for the topsy-turvy sensation it brought to his gut. It bothered him knowing she didn't feel like it was safe to talk to him. "I'm trying to be supportive."

"I'm not asking you to be supportive. I know you're not trying to make me feel bad. But, Marc, I have plans and dreams, too. I don't think I can be transparent about them with you."

"What if I try harder?"

"That's just the thing." She sighed, shaking her head. "I don't want you to have to try harder. I just want…"

"What, Reagan?" He reached for her hand and caressed it with his thumb. "What do you want?"

"I want to be important enough to you that you don't have to try."

It had cost her a lot to admit it. He could tell by the way her lips pinched together and how she wouldn't meet his eyes.

"You are important to me. I just…"

"Don't." She shook her head. "I think I want too much."

At that, he dropped her hand. Shame ripped through him. Reagan expected nothing from him or his family, and she'd sacrificed her time for weeks to help them out.

"You don't want too much. You deserve to feel important."

She flashed him a surprised glance. "I don't want to just *feel* important. I want to *be* important. Why else would I give my heart to someone?"

And that was when it hit him. He trusted her with everything, and she didn't trust him back. She *couldn't* trust him back. He'd made it impossible for her.

"You are important, Reagan. You're important to me." He shifted closer to her. "Can't you give me a chance?"

Her tongue darted out to moisten her upper lip. Was she scared of getting hurt? He knew the feeling well.

"I don't know. I want to, but I have a funny feeling about it."

"What do you mean?" He straightened his shoulders.

"I already explained."

She had, but it wasn't enough. He wanted to

talk her out of her feelings. Wanted to convince her that the two of them could work.

But, at the end of the day, she was right. There was an invisible wall separating them, and until he made peace with the fact she was opening her shop in the building his mother wanted, he doubted the wall could come down.

Friday afternoon, Reagan finished unpacking the tower of boxes she'd discovered on her front porch after returning from Marc's ranch. She'd helped Brooke with the twins again today until Anne had finished up at the bakery. She had to admit it was nice getting to know Marc's sister. They'd bonded over the babies, but they'd also opened up about their losses; Brooke's with Ross and Reagan's with Cody. For only knowing the woman a short time, Reagan felt remarkably close to her.

She was getting too involved with Marc's family. The babies were so dear to her, she actually didn't like thinking about not spending time with them regularly once Brooke no longer needed help. And then there was Marc…

Loyal, hardworking, self-sacrificing and so incredibly handsome.

If he'd just let her into his inner circle, he'd realize how good they could be together. But, for whatever reason, he wouldn't. It hurt knowing that he wouldn't be happy for her when she opened the store.

She hadn't heard yet if her building permit was approved, but she figured it probably took some time. The thought of moving forward with her plans kept bringing a strange mix of excitement along with hesitation, and she wasn't sure why.

Was it Marc? Was it normal nerves? She didn't know.

She cut the tape on the box from a gourmet chocolate supplier and opened it. Pouches of various chocolates had been packed inside, and she took them out one by one. Would it hurt to open each bag and breathe in their delectable scents? Not yet. Instead, she lined them on her countertop, took a photo and just stared in wonder.

This was happening. She *was* starting her company. She *was* creating her own chocolates.

Leaving her lovely bags of chocolate on the counter, she went to the box that held one of the tempering machines she'd purchased. All of the specialty chocolates she'd learned to make danced in front of her eyes. It had been almost a month since she'd made any treats, and she missed it.

The urge to experiment couldn't be ignored. But what to start with? The rich cherry ganache she'd been playing around with in Denver came to mind. It would taste like a chocolate-covered cherry, but it would be less messy, more refined. Marc was sure to love it, since he'd mentioned that chocolate-covered cherries were his favorite.

Oh, Marc.

Things had been distant between them since their heart-to-heart after Brooke came home.

Had she been wrong to tell him how she felt? Maybe she shouldn't have been quite so honest with him.

She wasn't any good at romance. Other women made it look so easy. They seemed to know how to flirt. They knew what to say and how to get guys to notice them.

Then there was her. Unable—or unwilling—to flirt. Never really knowing what to say. No clue how to get a guy to notice her and too blunt for anything to develop if one did.

Maybe the timing was off anyhow. Erica was right. Reagan had spent so much time and energy helping Marc with the twins, she'd begun to lose sight of what was important to her.

Blowing out a breath, she eyed all of the supplies now lining her kitchen counters. Then her attention wandered to the walls—the boring taupe walls. She'd been living here for a month and there wasn't a stamp of her identity or her style anywhere to be found.

It was time to change that.

She repacked all of the supplies in the boxes, then stacked them along the wall in the dining room adjacent to the kitchen. As much as she itched to play around with her new toys and start dipping chocolates, practical matters came first.

A trip to the hardware store to get paint swatches was in order. Reagan found her athletic shoes, pulled on a lightweight jacket, grabbed her purse and headed outside. Before she descended the porch steps, she paused to consider the covered porch. The boards were in good shape, but they needed to be stained or painted, and the faded light gray paint on the columns and rails was chipping.

Another thing to tackle soon.

She skipped down the steps onto the curved sidewalk that led to the driveway and turned back to take in the house. It was a Craftsman-style, one-story bungalow with dark gray siding. Tilting her head, she studied it. The exterior would be more appealing if she had the porch and columns painted white. With a little TLC, the house would pop. Plus, the porch needed some furniture and a wreath on the door to make it more inviting.

Reagan pivoted and made her way down the sidewalk toward Center Street. Her to-do list for the house was growing. Before today, it had all felt too overwhelming to think about. But now, for whatever reason, she was ready.

As soon as she finished selecting the paint swatches, she was going home, taking out the tempering machine and testing the chocolate she'd bought.

R. Mayer Chocolates, here we come!

In and out. He'd be back home before he knew it. That was what he'd told himself when his mom had handed him a list of things to buy for the twins. Marc had memorized the baby aisle of the grocery store at this point. It wasn't as if they were in desperate need of diapers. His mom was back to micromanaging everything, and he didn't mind. The sooner they were all back to normal, the better.

Marc tossed the bags into the back seat of his truck, shut the door and stood there with his face to the sky. The fresh air grounded him. With Trevor on duty at the ranch and his mom, sister and the twins doing okay, he realized he didn't want to return home right now. In fact, he wouldn't mind a break from the place.

He stepped up into the truck and fired the engine. How long had it been since he'd done anything for himself? If it didn't involve the ranch, the planning commission, the legacy club, his mother, his sister or the babies, he didn't take the time for it.

Maybe he needed to make time for his life.

There was only one thing he wanted to do on a fine Friday night like this.

Visit Reagan.

He backed the truck out of the spot and turned onto Center Street. He missed her. Hadn't spoken to her since their conversation yesterday. He'd already been out checking cattle when she'd arrived this morning, and she'd left before he was finished for the day.

Sure, he could have waited until she'd gotten there to talk to her, but he hadn't. He'd been mad at himself. Because she was right. He'd made the topic of her building off-limits. And he didn't see it changing anytime soon.

The thought of his mom's dream never being fulfilled hurt in a way he couldn't put into words. He wanted his mom to be happy. So much had been taken from her. Was it wrong of him to want her to have what she deserved? Just once in her life?

After Reagan's permit was approved, his mom's vision for her expanded bakery would be over. He'd have to get used to the thought. Because Reagan showed no signs of changing her mind. He didn't have the heart to try to change it anymore, either.

He'd just have to get over it.

Soon, he was pulling into her driveway. As he got out, he took in the neighborhood. The street was lined with older bungalows. Her house held no personal touches, no welcoming decorations. He climbed the porch steps. Not even a welcome mat.

It hit him again how much time she'd spent helping him and his family when she could have been working on her own home, her own plans. Without overthinking it, he knocked. And looked over his shoulder as he waited. She might not be home. He knocked again.

The door opened, and Reagan's eyes grew round as she smiled. "What are you doing here?"

"I was in the neighborhood." His spirits lifted at the warm glow of the light behind her and the sound of relaxing music from inside.

"Come in." She held the door open, and he brushed past her, wanting to pause and take her hand in his. As he looked in her eyes, all he could think was how much he wouldn't mind kissing her.

He forced his feet forward, and she locked the door behind her. It smelled amazing in here, like walking smack-dab into a brownie.

"I'm in the middle of trying out some new equipment." She padded confidently to the kitchen and pointed to the stools at the U-shaped butcher-block counter. "Have a seat."

She stood on the other side of it and pulled on a pair of plastic gloves. Then she selected a small oval of what looked like cookie dough, balanced it on two upturned fingers, dipped it into a machine with melted chocolate, shook off the excess and flipped her fingers over to set it on a parchment-paper-lined tray. She did a little swirly thing with her finger on the top of it.

"What are you making?" After taking a seat, he let his elbows drop onto the counter and craned his neck to peek at the chocolate. What he wouldn't give to dip a finger into that chocolate and have a lick.

"Vanilla buttercreams." She was already midway through dipping another chocolate. "I wanted to see how the new chocolate-tempering machine works. Then I found myself whipping up a batch of buttercream centers, and by the time the chocolate was melted, the centers were chilled, and here I am."

"You do them all by hand?" he asked.

"For the most part. I pour the barks into molds, and I have a few specialty chocolates I use molds for as well."

"What happens after they're all dipped?" His

mouth watered as more candies joined the others on the tray.

"They get chilled. I wish I had my temperature-controlled displays. My refrigerator is too cold. But these are just samples anyway. Go ahead and try one if you want."

He didn't need to be told twice. He reached over and popped one in his mouth. The chocolate hit him right away. Then the light texture of the cream and the rich vanilla flavor burst through right after.

It was the best chocolate he'd ever eaten.

"Wow." He eyed the rest of the tray. "That was delicious."

"Thank you." Her smile lit her eyes. "Have more. I don't want them to go to waste."

"What other kinds do you normally make?" he asked as he selected another one.

"The chocolatier who taught me had a set selection he kept on hand all the time. He added new items for the various holidays. I'm going to use a similar strategy, but I haven't settled on the exact chocolates I'll choose to be my regulars."

As she finished dipping the batch, she explained about the types of chocolates and caramels she liked to make. When she was done, she selected one of the chocolates and took a bite, then chewed with a thoughtful expression.

He wasn't sure what she was experiencing with her bite, but from the way one eye narrowed, he guessed it wasn't the taste-bud explosion he'd had.

"I was afraid of that. It needs more vanilla. I'll have to order vanilla beans and make my own extract."

"Really? I thought it was amazing."

It must have pleased her because she gave him a shy shrug. "I appreciate that." Then she began cleaning up. He offered to help, but she laughed and claimed there wasn't room for both of them. She had a point. They chatted about the twins as she tidied the counters and cleaned the equipment. When she was done, she wiped her hands dry on a kitchen towel.

"Have you eaten supper?" he asked.

"No." Her nose scrunched. "I haven't thought that far ahead."

"Do you want to order a pizza? Cowboy John's is the best." He tensed, waiting for her response.

"Sounds good to me."

"I'll order us one. What do you want on it?" He almost tripped as he got off the stool and searched through the contacts on his phone.

"Do they have a supreme? I like all the toppings."

"They do." He called in the order, then put his

phone in his pocket and stood there awkwardly. "I like your house."

"I haven't done much with it." She began walking to the living room and waved for him to follow her. "It's more comfortable in here."

He passed into a cozy living room. A brick fireplace took up part of one wall. The dark gray sectional and matching chair and ottoman looked new. The end tables were bare except for lamps and a tissue box. A large television in the corner had him grinning. Big televisions meant good viewing when football season came back around.

"I still need to decorate." She sat on one end of the sectional and curled her legs under her body. "I finally got over to the hardware store earlier for paint swatches."

"Oh, yeah? What colors are you thinking?" He sat at the other end and shifted to face her better.

"I'll show you." She scrambled to her feet and left the room. She was back within seconds. After resuming her spot on the couch, she handed him the swatches and scooted over to the cushion next to him, pointing to the squares in his hand. "I like this one, but I think it will end up too pastel in here. I should go with a darker shade."

"The darker shade would look good in here."

He couldn't think straight with her this close to him.

"You think so? I could decorate with these accent colors." She shuffled through the swatches until she found the ones she was looking for.

"Accent colors, huh?" He didn't know much about those.

"Yeah, for pillows and throws and little items for the mantel." A dreamy expression crossed her face as she leaned in even closer to him and tucked her legs under once more. He could smell her perfume, along with a lingering chocolate aroma. Her hair was *this* close to his shoulder. It would be so simple to reach out and touch it. "It will feel more like home when I decorate it."

Even in its undecorated state, something about it felt like home to him now. He wasn't sure if it was the chocolate, the background music or Reagan herself, but he found himself relaxing more with every second that passed. The general sense of calm had been missing in his life for quite some time.

"Do you ever get nervous?" He inched his hand toward hers until their fingers touched. "Living by yourself in a new town?"

She didn't move her hand away. "A little. But not too much. I know if anything goes wrong, Erica and Dalton would be here in a snap."

"You can call me, too, you know." He wanted

to be the one she called. Wanted to protect her, to help her, to fix anything she needed.

"I know."

Their eyes met and the urge to touch her was so strong, he no longer fought it. He tenderly touched her cheek, then pushed a lock of hair behind her ear.

"I want to kiss you, Reagan. Tell me I shouldn't." His voice was low; his gaze locked on her lips.

She shook her head, her eyes golden, and he didn't hesitate. He pressed his lips to hers. They were soft. So soft. Tender, like her personality. He needed this.

He needed her.

His hands cupped her face as he deepened the kiss. Sensations swirled. She tasted like chocolate, and her skin was smooth, satiny. His heart pounded. Impressions flashed.

Reagan was sunshine, determination, hope and joy.

How in just a few weeks' time had she become so necessary to him?

The doorbell rang, and he reluctantly let her go. He searched her eyes and was reassured by what he saw in them. She didn't hate him, that was for sure.

"Pizza's here." The corner of her mouth quirked up.

He stood and bent to kiss her one more time. "I'll take care of it."

He wanted to be the one who took care of anything she needed. He wanted to be the guy who took care of her.

As he approached the front door, questions swam to the surface. What if he couldn't? What if he didn't have enough to give? What if he tried and ended up neglecting his mother, sister and the twins in the process?

Marc opened the front door. He'd worry about all that another time. This was the first Friday night he'd enjoyed himself in ages. He planned to make the most of it and get the big answers later.

Chapter Eleven

How was it possible she still hadn't gotten any word on her building permit?

Over a week later, on Monday morning, Reagan checked her phone, but there weren't any missed calls or texts from Ed or Henry. There was a text from her mom. A picture of her nieces in matching sundresses and cowboy boots. She was definitely having that one printed and framed. But even their adorableness couldn't distract her from this antsy sensation.

It had been ten days—but who was counting?—since Marc had stopped by so unexpectedly. The pizza had been delicious. The company? Phenomenal. And the kiss? Had been everything she'd dreamed Hot Cowboy's kiss would be and more. She hadn't stopped thinking about it…or him.

She let out a happy sigh and returned to the

task at hand—making chocolates for Clem and Slim. She dipped a monster of a strawberry into the chocolate. Today was the first day she hadn't gone out to Marc's ranch to help with the babies. One of Brooke's friends had offered to help with the twins all week. As much as Reagan enjoyed taking care of the girls, it had been nice to sleep in and sip coffee in her pj's on the couch for as long as she'd wanted this morning.

Would Marc call her later? He'd been making an extra effort with her since their kiss. Each morning when she arrived at the ranch, he lingered over his coffee to chat. And when his mother arrived in the afternoon, he would meet Reagan outside as she headed to her car. They'd talk for a while. On Wednesday afternoon, they'd even toured the ranch on horseback. Reagan had always loved riding—as long as it was slow. She'd never been the galloping or rodeo-competing type. Then, Thursday, on a whim, she'd invited Marc over for supper.

It had been so nice, so easy. She'd made tacos, and they'd talked about all kinds of things. Childhood memories. Favorite foods. Movies they liked. And they'd gone deeper, too. About how hard life had been for him after his dad had left them. And she'd shared how much pain she'd felt when Cody cut off all communication from the family in the months before he died.

Over the years, she'd made peace with it, but every now and then she still wondered if she could have done more.

Marc made her feel safe. He listened without giving advice—unheard of in the family she'd grown up in—and he made her feel interesting, pretty, even talented. All the things her family had assured her she was, but until she'd met Marc, she hadn't quite believed.

The only problem? He still couldn't bring himself to discuss her building. Instead, they tiptoed around the subject. At some point, it would come to a head, and they'd either continue exploring their relationship or it would end in a spectacular explosion.

She hated explosions. Wasn't a fan of conflict, in general.

Reagan dipped and swirled the strawberry, then set it on the parchment-lined tray with the others. Slim was going to love these. They'd met for an hour earlier this week to tie up loose ends. He'd simplified everything, and she appreciated his patience with her. Even Erica was impressed with all the progress she'd made with Slim's help.

As she dipped another strawberry, her mind went back to the corner building and all the changes she and Ed had discussed. She had no doubt it would be welcoming and lovely when it was all said and done. But she could still see the vision of her chocolate shop in the bakery. And that was the one she continued to dream about.

Reagan lifted the lid on the square metal container of pink-colored white chocolate in one of the melting machines. It looked ready. She drizzled it over the chocolate-covered strawberries, then repeated the process with the red-colored white chocolate.

Why did she keep thinking about the bakery? Was it simply a distraction? Or was it more?

She shook her head. Too late now. She'd signed the contract with McCaffrey Construction. It made no sense to be fantasizing about a much smaller building tucked into the heart of downtown. Easily missed. Easily passed by.

But she kept seeing the floating shelves she'd install on the wall to the left of the entrance, and the entire front wall replaced with glass, bringing in light and allowing anyone walking past to see inside.

She wiped her hands on her apron. Why was she doing this to herself? Why was she fantasizing about the wrong building?

If she asked anyone—right here, right now— if it made more sense to open R. Mayer Chocolates in her building or in the space where Annie's Bakery currently resided, they would laugh out loud and tell her the corner building. No question.

And if Erica or her mother knew the thoughts she was having, they'd blame it on her growing attraction to Marc. They'd tell her she was falling in love. That she was only having these fantasies about the bakery because she knew it would make Marc happy.

Would they be right?

She didn't know. And she didn't want to examine it too closely.

She'd stick to her plan. It was too late to back out now even if she wanted to. And the truth was, she didn't know what she wanted. All she knew was that whatever was growing between her and Marc felt precious...and she didn't want it to end.

"Hey, Marc, you got a minute?"

"Sure. What's going on?" Marc paused as Henry Zane came out of his office at city hall Monday. Marc had just finished catching up on work for the planning and zoning commission. He hadn't had much time to deal with it since Brooke's stroke.

Henry's cheeks were red and he seemed flustered as he approached. He waved the paperwork in his hand. "Could you do me a favor?

See that this gets to Reagan Mayer. She's still helping out with the twins at your ranch, right?"

"Most days, yes."

"Great." The man's face relaxed in relief. "I'm running late, and Angie'll have my head if I even think about canceling our trip to the city this afternoon. The permit slipped my mind last week, and I don't want Reagan to have to wait another day. Ed's out of town, too, or I'd give it to him."

Marc's lungs compressed, and a funny feeling rose up from his feet to his head—a hard feeling. Like he was turning to stone as Henry spoke. He'd known this day was coming, but he'd been putting it off, trying to pretend it would be okay.

And all he could see was his mom's pale, pinched face on the day the divorce was final. She'd turned to Marc and said so softly he'd almost missed it, "He could have left me before your grandma died. He waited one week after the funeral to tell me he was leaving. It's like he was waiting to take my inheritance."

"You okay?" Henry gave him a questioning look.

"Yes. Fine." He thrust his hand out to take the papers from him. "I'll take care of it."

"Great. You tell her if she has any questions, I'll be in my office on Wednesday."

"Will do." Marc nodded goodbye and marched down the hall, through the front entrance and straight to his truck. Once inside, he tossed the permit onto the passenger seat and just sat there.

What was he going to tell his mother? It wasn't like she didn't know Reagan was opening a chocolate shop in the corner building. She did. Everyone in town knew about it. But he hadn't brought up the subject, and neither had she. They'd been focused on Brooke and Megan and Alice.

But they'd also been helpless to change the situation, and maybe that had held them back, too. Sometimes he felt like the only thing that had gotten his mom through those rough early years in her tiny bakery was her dream of expanding—and not any old spot would do. The goal had always been the corner building.

And now he had to go tell Reagan that *her* dream was about to come true at the expense of his mother's. As much as he cared about Reagan, as much as he craved her company, as much as he enjoyed being with her and respected her, he didn't think she wanted that building as badly as his mother did.

His breathing grew shallow as scenarios raced through his head. Would his mom blame him for not talking Reagan out of it? Would she hold a grudge against Reagan?

He'd grown so close to her, was falling harder for her every day. What if it caused tension in his family? If his mother and sister resented Reagan, how could he in fairness offer her anything more than friendship?

Pull yourself together. He started the truck and drove away.

He'd give Reagan the permit and talk to his mom later. She was mature. She'd handle it. But it would break her heart, and he'd already seen that heart broken before.

It took less than five minutes to get to Reagan's house. As he got out of his truck, he tried to come up with something to say that would be appropriate, but words failed him.

His footsteps slowed the closer he got, and by the time he'd made it up the porch steps and knocked on her door, there was a sour taste in his mouth and his body felt heavy.

The door opened and Reagan beamed at him. She was so beautiful, he could only stare. Her beauty shone from within, and he wanted so badly to be the man she needed right now. It would be the easiest thing in the world to hand her the permit and take her in his arms and congratulate her with a kiss. To take her out to supper to celebrate. Let her tell him everything she knew about chocolates for as long as her heart desired.

But he couldn't work his mouth into a smile. Couldn't muster a whisper of enthusiasm.

"What's wrong? Did something happen?" She frowned as she stepped onto the porch in front of him. "Is it Brooke? The babies?"

"Nothing's wrong." Shame washed over him as it registered that her first thoughts were for his family. "It's good news." His voice sounded strangled.

"It is?"

"Yes. Henry Zane asked me to drop this off to you." He handed her the papers, not taking his gaze off her face. "Your permit. Congratulations."

She scanned the top paper quickly, and a smile flashed, then disappeared.

"Thank you for dropping it off."

"Sure thing." He backed up a step, letting his head drop. *Just leave. Go home. Don't make this worse.* "I'll leave you to celebrate."

Reagan didn't answer, and when he glanced at her, her expression brimmed with hurt.

"I'll just go." He started to turn.

"Wait."

He gave her his full attention.

"Why can't you let me have this?" she asked quietly. "It's my career. I do want to celebrate. I'd like to celebrate it with you, but I know better."

He swallowed and shifted his jaw. "You won. Let's leave it at that."

"Won?" Her nose scrunched in confusion. "This wasn't a competition. It's not a game with winners and losers."

"Tell that to my mom." He opened his hands. "Because she's lost an awful lot over the years."

"I'm not the one who took anything from her."

"You kind of did."

"Is that how you see it?" She raised herself to full height, which was still several inches shorter than he was. "Your mother never owned the corner building. It was never hers. And it is mine. I own it."

"You inherited it."

"Yeah, so?" Her face was growing splotchy and he hated that he was doing this. This conversation was all wrong, and yet he couldn't stop making it worse. "It's still mine."

"She deserves it."

A breeze rippled between them, and the light in her eyes went dark. She stepped back, crossing her arms over her chest. "And I don't. Got it."

Now he really did feel like the world's biggest jerk. "I didn't say that."

"Marc, you've said it in so many words since the day we met. I just chose to ignore it. But we both know it's there."

He ground his teeth together, unable to deny it.

"I'm never going to be as important to you as your mom and your sister. I won't even be as important to you as the twins. And I deserve better than that." At the pain in her voice, his heart clenched. Were those tears in her eyes? "I think you should leave."

"Reagan…" He reached out to touch her arm, but she jerked it away, shaking her head. "You're important to me. You are."

"Not enough. I'm…" She blinked away the tears. "I'm not okay with this. I thought we had something special, and my feelings for you are real. I don't give my heart to anyone lightly, and I'm not giving it to someone who can't be happy for me. So why don't you just get out of here? I'm done."

Before he could say another word, she'd stepped back inside the house. The loud slam of the door rattled him. He stalked down the porch steps to his truck. Roared out of her drive and onto the street.

He was furious. Not with Reagan. With himself.

Because every word she'd said was true. And he hated himself for it.

Reagan leaned her back against the front door as tremors rippled through her body. *No regrets, no regrets.*

She was full of regrets.

And she'd do it all again in a heartbeat. She'd offer to babysit the twins. She'd get to know Marc. She'd sit on her couch and discuss paint swatches and let him kiss her. Yes, she'd do it all.

Still, how could she have been so delusional? Here she'd thought Marc cared about her. She'd hoped he'd eventually move past the problem of the corner building.

But she'd been wrong. Oh, so wrong.

And now what was she going to do about Brooke and the twins? She wanted to help out, but the entire family would probably hate her by morning.

What did they want her to do? Hand over the deed to Anne with a "you had mental dibs on it, so it's yours"? Wasn't happening.

She pushed away from the door and grabbed her keys and purse. There was no way she was sitting here alone and crying for hours. This situation called for her best friend. Erica would know what to say. Erica would know what to do. Erica would feed her Gemma's coffee cake and let her cry to her heart's content.

Fifteen minutes later—yes, she'd exceeded the speed limit and didn't care—she pulled into Erica's ranch and ran up to her front door. Erica opened it immediately, took one look at her and dragged her inside.

"What's wrong? What happened?"

"I got my permit." The words were choppy.

"That's good news."

"Marc didn't think so." And then the tears came. Erica hugged her until the sobs subsided, then led her down the hall into the kitchen.

"Have a seat." She practically forced Reagan onto a stool at the huge island. "I'll brew the coffee."

Reagan dug in her purse for a tissue, and there was so much stuff in there, it made her cry even harder. "I can't even find a tissue. I'm such a mess. No wonder I'm still single."

"What?" Erica dismissed her with a wave. "That's not true. You are not a mess. And if you weren't at Marc's ranch all the time, I guarantee the single guys around here would be lining up to ask you on a date."

"No one has ever lined up to ask me for a date." Reagan was trying to pull herself together, but she hiccuped through the entire sentence. "Guys don't like me. And I thought Marc did, but I'm nothing to him, and I was stupid for thinking he might be the one."

"You're not stupid. You're smart and beautiful and kind and creative." Erica finished starting the pot of coffee and left the room momentarily.

She returned with a box of tissues that she set in front of Reagan. "Here."

"His entire family is going to hate me." She pulled three tissues out at warp speed and proceeded to wipe her eyes and blow her nose with them.

"What? No. They love you. You've been such a help to them."

"I'm not going to be able to help with the twins, and Brooke and I were starting to become friends."

Her sister moved to the other side of the island and took mugs out of the cupboard. "Is that what you're worried about? The twins?"

Was that what she was worried about? "No. I can handle being cut out of their lives. It'll hurt, though, and I really do want to get closer to Brooke."

"But?" Erica unwrapped a plate filled with blueberry muffins and lemon-drizzle pound cake.

"But getting over Marc is going to be hard." She'd kept her growing feelings for him to herself, and acknowledging them now was both painful and a relief.

Erica inhaled quickly and pointed her finger at Reagan. "You fell in love with him."

Had she? She squirmed, averting her eyes to the counter.

"And that jerk had the nerve to make you feel bad about getting the permit for a building *you own*?" The last two words seemed to boom through the air. "To think I thought he'd be good for you. And what does he do? Put his mother first. Like your shop doesn't matter. Who does he think he is? He doesn't own the store." Erica continued muttering all the things Reagan, too, had been thinking. She poured cream into the mugs, followed by steaming hot coffee, then set one of them in front of Reagan. "Don't worry. It's decaf."

The mug had swirly words spelling I Can't Even.

I can't even. Exactly. And Reagan gave in to another round of tears.

"Here, have a piece of Gemma's lemon-drizzle cake. It's melt-in-your-mouth good." Erica shoved the plate her way, and Reagan selected a small slice. "If you want to know what I think, he should be on his knees thanking you for all you've done for his family. He should personally be offering to help you remodel the building. He should be shouting to the hills how wonderful you are."

The lemon-drizzle slice fell out of her hand to the counter. Wouldn't that have been nice? To have him appreciate her? Be supportive of her? Offer to help her?

She'd fallen in love with the wrong guy.

Erica's right. I fell in love with him. How stupid could I be?

"Why don't you tell me everything?" Erica perched on a stool kitty-corner from Reagan and glued her attention to her. "Did you two kiss?"

Her cheeks were hotter than the scalding coffee she hadn't even attempted to sip.

"You did!" Erica reached over for a muffin. "Was this like an everyday thing? He'd come back from the ranch and see you with the twins, and he just couldn't help himself?"

"No! Nothing like that." The burst of indignation chased away the threat of tears. "It's just… we've gotten to know each other. We've been spending a lot of time together, and one night after Brooke came home, he stopped by. We ordered pizza and talked and…"

"He kissed you." Her eyes grew wide. The mug was practically dangling between her hands. "Go on."

"Over the past week or two, Marc and I have had more time to connect."

"Any red flags?"

"Only my building. Everything else is just right."

"But that's a big wrong."

"It is. It's the biggest wrong. I can't look past

it anymore. I tried. I just wouldn't mention the building. The funny thing is, he had no problem talking about the chocolate."

"You felt like you had to hide something important. Oh, Reag, I hate that for you."

"I do, too. I should have known better. I *knew* the topic bothered him. I knew how much he wanted his mother to have the building. I shouldn't have let myself get close to him."

Erica lifted one shoulder. "You're better than me. I always get too close."

"But you don't put up with any nonsense."

"Come on. You and I both know that isn't true. I put up with mountains of nonsense when I was married to Jamie. Dalton is different. He's no nonsense in the best possible way."

"I wish I could have what you guys have." It was hard for her to admit it. "I wish I was savvy like you and smarter and had just the right comeback when people are rude."

"Me? No. You're way better. You're kind to everyone. Your creativity astounds me. You have more talent than I could ever hope for."

"But I had to get help with every tiny business detail. And I knew Marc resented me because of the building, but I ignored it. How dumb."

Erica reached over and squeezed her hand. "We all get help with things we're not good at. That's normal. And I ignored a lot of things I shouldn't have with Jamie and even a few things with Dalton. We're human. It's okay."

"Thanks." Her shoulders slumped, and she took another sip of coffee. Nibbled on a bite of the lemon cake. It really was melt-in-your-mouth good.

"You know, Marc is kind of a mystery." Erica tapped her fingernail on the side of the mug. "From what I've been told, he'd never gotten serious with a woman around here. Doesn't really date much, either."

Reagan gave her a glum glance. "So?"

"So, you're the first woman who's gotten this far with him."

"Well, another woman will have to get him over the finish line. I'm done with him."

She was, too. She only had a few rules about dating. No cheating. Mutual respect. And she refused to be anything less than number one in his life.

Two out of three wasn't good enough. And she wasn't changing her mind. She and Marc were through. For good.

Chapter Twelve

"Mom, we have to talk." Marc waited for his mother to get settled on the couch later that night. Brooke had gone to bed half an hour ago, and the twins had been asleep for a while. This conversation needed to be between the two of them with no interruptions. And it had been gnawing at him ever since he'd left Reagan's place.

"What's going on?" She unfolded a fuzzy throw blanket and spread it over her legs.

"Reagan's building permit was approved today." He leaned forward in the recliner so he'd have a full view of her face. She nodded, then closed her eyes as her shoulders began to shake in silent sobs.

He went to her side, sat next to her and put his arm around her shoulders. He'd known this would be hard.

"I'm sorry, Mom."

She turned to him, wrapping her arms around him. He held her while she cried. Then she took a shaky breath and pulled herself together.

"I guess it's really over," she said. "The dream is over."

He wanted to tell her it wasn't over, that he'd find a way…but he couldn't.

"I wish I could have changed her mind," he said. "I tried, but I didn't try hard enough."

"No, Marc—" she shook her head "—this isn't Reagan's fault. She has her dreams, too. It's just… I'd put so much stock into mine."

"You deserve to open your bakery there. You had every right to dream about it."

She gave him a shrug that broke his heart. "It's not the first time I've had to let go of a dream. It will be okay. I'll just keep the bakery where it is and—"

"It's too small. It's always been too small." He ran his hand over his hair. "And if Dad hadn't taken everything, you wouldn't have had to open it in the first place."

"I'll always be glad I opened the bakery. I'm proud of my work."

"I know." He sighed. "I didn't mean to imply…"

"It's okay. I know what you meant. And your father didn't take everything," she said quietly.

"How can you say that?" His voice rose. "He made you sell off so much land. He took Grandma's assets, and he had no right to them. No right at all."

"I had you and Brooke. I kept half of the assets."

"*Your* assets."

"Legally, both of ours." She shrugged. "I survived. We survived."

"Yeah, and it was hard. You shouldn't have had to go through all that. Months of barely any sleep, worrying if we would lose this place. Loans and hard work and trying to settle accounts until business picked up. Your dream of moving the bakery should have come true. I wanted to make it come true."

"God provided for us."

"He hasn't done a very good job lately." He regretted it as soon as he said it, but he could no longer deny his feelings.

"How can you say that?" Her forehead creased.

"Brooke lost the love of her life. Then she had a stroke. You both had to move back here. I know how much that cost you. It hasn't been easy driving all the way to town before sunrise. I just wanted you to have this. I wanted the building to be yours."

"Life isn't easy. And, yes, Brooke lost Ross. She also had a stroke. But she has beautiful twin baby girls. She has a big brother who moved her back home and helps take care of her and the girls' needs. She's working hard to recover. You can see how well she gets around. We need to be thankful for that."

"I am thankful." Not thankful enough, obviously.

"She could have died. Have you considered that?"

"Of course I've considered it! I thought of nothing else the week she was in the hospital."

"Then stop looking at the negatives and focus on the positives. We have our Brooke back. That's all that really matters."

He clamped his mouth shut. While his mom was right about Brooke, other things mattered, too, and he couldn't pretend they didn't.

"I prayed for over fifteen years for that building, Marc, and it's time for me to accept that God has other plans for it. I'll move on. I will. Don't worry about me." She got to her feet and stood in front of him. "I'm glad Reagan is putting something special in the building. We need to be happy for her. Look at all she's done for us."

"Happy for her?" What was his mom thinking? "I'm not happy for her."

She gave him a sharp look. "What do you mean? I have eyes. I can see you two have been getting close."

"Not anymore."

"She's good for you. She's the first woman

you've let in—even a sliver. I hope you aren't pushing her away because of the building."

"I can't get past it. I need time. I'm too upset to even think straight at the moment."

"I love you, Marc. I want you to be happy. I want to see you settled. Reagan is good for you. Why would you push her away?"

"All these years, all you've talked about is expanding your bakery. And I told her how important it was to you."

"You can't expect her to toss out her plans for me. That's ridiculous."

"It's not ridiculous. Your dream is important. You're important. You and Brooke and Megan and Alice. All of you. Your happiness is important to me." The words came out more rapidly than he'd intended.

His mom frowned, tilted her head and studied him. He wasn't sure what she saw, but it didn't seem to be good.

"Marc, you've put our family first for over fifteen years. Maybe I expected too much from you. Maybe I put too much pressure on you. But my happiness has never been your responsibility. Nor has Brooke's. And don't get me started on the twins. We're all responsible for our own happiness."

He wanted to refute her but, as the words sank in, he couldn't.

"What's really going on with you? What are you afraid of?"

That you'll see I failed you and you'll leave me. Just like Dad did. I should have done more. Should have been more. Then he wouldn't have left and taken so much of what mattered to us.

He sat in the chair, propped his elbows on his knees and let his forehead fall into his hands.

"Honey, I love you. I'll get over my disappointment about the bakery. All those times we discussed expanding it filled me with optimism. But I never intended to make you feel responsible for making it happen."

"I know you didn't. I put it on myself."

"You've put a lot on yourself over the years, haven't you?" The words came out softly. "Maybe too much. Maybe Brooke and the girls should move to town with me. It might be easier for all of us."

"No!" He couldn't believe his mom was threatening to move out. "This is exactly what I was afraid would happen."

"What are you talking about?"

"I couldn't get the building for you, and now you're threatening to cut me out of your life just like Dad did!" As soon as the words left his mouth, he froze, stunned at the realization he actually believed it.

All these years, he'd never allowed himself to

face his worst fears. And here they were. Tumbling out of his mouth.

"I would never cut you out of my life. Never." Mom cupped his cheek with her hand, and the outpouring of love from her eyes brought his anxiety down a notch. "Nothing you do could ever make me not love you. You and Brooke are my life. It would be like cutting out my heart. You've never had to earn my love. It's yours. It's always been yours."

As the words seeped in, he felt a sense of peace that had been missing since he was sixteen.

"I only suggested Brooke moving because it's a lot having us all here. You deserve to have your own life, too."

"You guys are my life, Ma."

She patted his arm. "I know. I'm blessed. But there's room in your life for one more. Don't shut Reagan out because of us."

He didn't respond. Couldn't respond.

He'd already shut Reagan out. He didn't see a way back in.

Even if he did, he wasn't sure he was ready. It was easy for Mom to talk about making room for one more, but he'd already burned his bridges with Reagan and, unlike his mom and sister, he doubted she'd be able to overlook his shortcomings.

He'd fallen in love with her. And he'd hurt her. Chosen his mom's happiness over hers.

He never should have gotten close to Reagan Mayer. He'd known all along it would end badly. And it had.

The twenty-four-hour rule for hosting a pity party had come and gone, and Reagan was no closer to moving off her couch and changing out of her stretched-out, faded leggings than she'd been yesterday. She didn't care, either. So what if it was late Wednesday morning? She didn't have a job. Didn't have any place to be.

A fresh batch of sadness whipped up to fill her heart.

If she had her way, she'd be with Brooke and the twins right this minute. She'd be telling Megan stories and kissing Alice's little cheeks. She'd be breathlessly anticipating the moment when Marc would join her in the driveway so they could catch up the way he had before he'd given her the permit.

But, no. Brooke had the baby help covered this week, and who knew what would happen after that? Marc hadn't reached out. No texts, no calls, no apologies. So why did she keep checking her phone?

Earlier, she'd gotten four texts and one phone call. The texts, in order, had been from Erica, her mom, Erica again, and the final one had been a reminder for a dental cleaning back in Sunrise Bend she'd forgotten to cancel. The phone call had been from Ed McCaffrey to let her know he'd be back in town on Monday to go over the timeline of her project.

As if she even cared at this point.

She wasn't sure if Marc had permanently tainted the corner building for her or if her irrational vision for opening her store in his mom's bakery was the culprit. Either way, the thought of renovating brought her no joy.

Her cell phone rang, and she kicked off the throw blanket tangled around her legs. Tripped as she got to her feet and lunged for the phone.

"Hello?"

"Hey, Reagan, how are you?" Her brother Blaine was on the line. He rarely called. She didn't want to panic, but her mind went straight to his two-month-old baby, Ethan.

"Is something wrong? Is it Ethan?"

"Nothing's wrong. Ethan's getting bigger every day. Wish he'd sleep a little more. Maddie's obsessed with him. Thinks he's her real-life doll." His chuckle calmed her nerves. She traced her steps back to her spot on the couch and sat down. "I haven't talked to you in a while. Thought I'd see how everything's going."

For years, Blaine had been her rock. Even before he'd married Sienna, he'd always included Reagan in his plans. She missed him. Right now, she missed her entire family, especially her mom, whom she'd talked to several times yesterday about the Marc situation.

"It's going." She didn't trust herself to say more without falling apart.

"You don't sound very happy."

"I'm not."

A long pause had her closing her eyes. She didn't want Blaine to worry, and he was the type to worry about her. But she also didn't want to hide anything from him.

"Is it serious?" he asked.

"Until a few days ago, it was going great here. I've been helping out with the cutest little babies—identical twin girls—I'm sure Mom has told you about them. And everything is moving along for the chocolate shop."

"What's wrong, then?" His low voice soothed her nerves.

"Everything." She fought back her emotions. "Marc, the twins' uncle, and I grew close, but he's not the right guy for me—"

"What did he do?" There was an edge to his tone.

"Nothing. He and I had different ideas on how my building should be used."

"What business is it of his? If this guy is bothering you, say the word and I'll leave right now to have a talk with him. In fact, I'll bring Jet with me."

Like that would go over well. Her two over-protective brothers riding into town to confront Marc? Her oldest brother, Jet, once had a stare-down with a classmate in high school who'd nicknamed her Scarecrow, and the kid had been so intimidated he'd avoided her in the halls from that day forward.

"No. It's not like that. His mom has always dreamed of moving her bakery into my building."

"I hope you told him 'too bad.' That's *your* building."

She let out a miserable sigh. "I did."

"Good."

"But, Blaine..." She'd always been able to confide in him. Out of all her family, Blaine was the safest person to tell how she really felt. "I don't know. Lately, I don't feel right about the building."

"That does it. I'm coming down there and talking to this guy myself. He cannot push you around."

She could feel a tension headache coming on. "He's not pushing me around. This feeling has nothing to do with him."

"Then what is it?" And that was why she loved Blaine. He was willing to listen.

"It doesn't feel right." Those four words brought relief. Admitting it—out loud—was like finding the key that fit.

"What doesn't feel right about it?" Anyone else in her family would have assured her she just had cold feet and that once the renovations were finished, it would be perfect. Not Blaine.

"It's bigger than I need. I have a floor plan that would be the envy of anyone opening a retail shop, yet all I can think about is this other building. It's half the size and wedged between two businesses. Makes no sense, I know. But when I go in there, I can picture my shop down to the tiniest details, from the floating shelves to where the display cases would go."

"Is it empty?"

"No, and this is where things get weird."

"I'm used to weird with you."

She chuckled. "Fair enough. Marc's mom's bakery is in there."

"The one that wants to expand into your building?"

"Yes."

"You're not giving yourself a consolation prize to win this guy over, are you?"

Was she? "I don't think so. In fact, I know I'm not."

"How can you be sure?"

"Because I broke it off with Marc on Monday."

"Is this your way of getting him back?"

"That's not it, either. I thought he could be the one, but I'm obviously not very important to him, and I'm not okay with that."

"Where did you get all your brains from?"

"We all know I'm not the brains of the family, Blaine."

"You're smart, and you mean the world to me, Reagan. Whatever you do, don't settle for second best. You're worth so much more."

Grateful tears pressed, and she took a moment to get grounded. "Thanks, Blaine."

"You'll know what to do. Trust your instincts."

Trust her instincts. She smiled to herself. Yes, that was why she'd moved here.

"I will."

"And if you need me to come down there and have a talk with this Marc guy, say the word."

"I'm good."

"Should I call Dalton to confront him?"

"No!"

"Okay, okay. I love you."

"I love you, too. Thanks for calling."

Talking to Blaine clarified things. She was growing more convinced every day that the corner building wasn't right for her shop.

Why couldn't she have figured all this out three weeks ago? She'd signed a contract with Ed. The renovations would be starting soon.

Even if she wanted Annie's Bakery, she had no idea if it was even possible for her to get it. Did Anne own the building? Lease it? What would be involved?

Dear Lord, I keep feeling like I'm hitting a roadblock when it comes to my plan. Will You help me figure out what to do?

One thing she knew. Marc *would* treat her differently if she decided to give up on the corner building. But it wouldn't matter. Because deep down she knew when push came to shove, she wasn't as important to him as he was to her. And that was a deal-breaker.

No matter where she opened her shop, she had no future with him.

Chapter Thirteen

"What's got you down, boss?" Rico asked Wednesday after lunch. "You're less fun to be around than a wasp in a closet."

"Nothing." Marc cranked the wrench harder to tighten the bolt. He'd just replaced a part in the old truck they used to haul water around the ranch. Did it need to be replaced today? No. But he was determined to keep his mind occupied.

"Yeah, right." A skeptical *psshh* escaped his lips. "The honeybuns okay?"

"They're fine."

"And their mama?"

"Also fine. She made it up half the staircase all by herself last night before she got tired and needed my help."

"Good. What about Miss Anne? She okay?"

"Yes. She's okay." Was she, though? He tightened the bolt with one more crank, then straightened and tossed the wrench back in the tool chest. His mom seemed to be back to her normal self after their conversation Monday night. But was she hiding her pain?

"Then it must be Twinkles."

"Twinkles?"

"Yeah, Reagan. Her eyes are always twinkling."

Reagan's eyes *were* always twinkling. She had an amazing attitude. He missed those eyes. Missed that attitude.

"I noticed her car hasn't been around."

"Yeah, well, Gracie's been coming over every morning to help Brooke with the twins."

Rico rolled the air compressor back to the corner. "Why don't you take a drive? Go see Twinkles."

"Nah. I've got to check the new calves."

"You checked them an hour ago."

"Then I'll make sure the—"

"Look, boss, I don't normally involve myself in other people's beeswax, but it's clear to me you need a shove."

No, he didn't.

"Move this back to the side of the shed, will you?" Marc tossed Rico the keys to the truck.

Rico caught them with one hand. "I will. After you hear me out."

He didn't want to listen to a single word anyone had to say. He just wanted to be left alone. Forever. Or at least until his heart stopped crinkling up like an old burger wrapper being thrown in the trash every time he thought about Reagan.

"That girl is good for you. You could have a nice life with her. Settle down. Have a couple honeybuns of your own."

"I know, okay? I know. I blew it." Was his throat lined with lighter fluid? One wrong word would ignite the whole thing.

"Last I heard, most couples fight."

"We didn't fight." He almost said they weren't a couple, but they had been. For a short time.

"Whatever you messed up can be fixed."

"Not this."

"I don't believe that."

"Believe it or don't. Doesn't matter to me. I was upset that she's opening her chocolate shop in Mom's building. And she knew it. I couldn't be supportive, so we're done."

Rico rubbed his chin and nodded thoughtfully. "I can see how that's a problem."

Marc's shoulders sagged. It was a problem.

"She thinks she's not important to me. And I take the blame for that. I'm still struggling with it. I wanted Mom's dream to come true."

"Go on."

He kicked at a cardboard box on the ground and instantly regretted it. Was it filled with cement? "It's all she's talked about for years, but Reagan is opening her chocolate shop there."

Rico's sigh irritated him.

"Why don't you leave it to the women to work it out?"

"There's no working it out. Reagan got her building permit. Hired a contractor. It's happening."

"Let me ask you something else." He brushed his hands down the sides of his jeans. "If you convinced her to give the building to your mama, could you live with yourself?"

"Of course. Why?"

"Because you'd be taking away Twinkles' dream. I've known you for a long time, boss. I don't think you'd feel so good about yourself if you did that."

Marc hadn't thought about that aspect. He hadn't really considered Reagan's point of view about her shop. He thought of all the times her face had glowed as she'd explained about how she'd learned to make truffles or her excitement at finding just the right chocolate to order. He'd loved listening to her. Loved being with her.

He loved her.

But how could he claim to love her when he'd purposely ignored what was important to her?

Chocolates were her passion. The building? She was right. She owned it. And he'd pressured her to step aside for his mother's sake. No matter what angle he looked at, the only conclusion he could come to was that Reagan was better off without him.

"I've got to go." He turned to leave.

"Go to town," Rico called. "Talk to her."

He wasn't going to town or talking to her. He was saddling up and taking a long ride. It was time to figure out how he'd become the kind of guy he loathed. The one who'd take away the dream of the woman he loved for his own selfish reasons.

Like father, like son.

There was no coming back from this.

Reagan was toweling off her hair when she heard a knock on her front door. It had been a few hours since her conversation with Blaine. During that time, she'd fixed herself a bowl of soup and asked herself what she wanted. The more she thought about it, the more she realized it didn't matter how far along with her plans she was—she needed to do what was right for her. And that meant talking to Marc's mother. Just the two of them. She'd call Anne tomorrow. Maybe by then she'd have a clue how to present her plan.

She tossed the towel into a hamper, then padded to the front door. Marc's mom stood on the doorstep.

"Anne." Reagan was taken aback. "Come in."

Was she here to try to convince her to let her have the building for her bakery? Reagan didn't like the thought of Anne, too, thinking her dream was more important than her own.

"Are you sure?" Her lips curved into a weak smile. "This isn't a bad time?"

"It's a good time. I have nothing going on." She held the door open wider for Marc's mom to come inside. She led the way to the living room.

"I like your house." Anne took in the room. "We're practically neighbors—well, we will be when I move back to town."

"Thank you. Have a seat." Reagan sat in one of the chairs as Anne perched on the couch. "Why are you here?"

"Marc doesn't know I came." Anne smoothed her hand over the throw pillow next to her, then met Reagan's gaze. "But I had to stop by for a couple of reasons. First, to thank you. The twins have been in good hands while Brooke recovered. Your generosity and kindness allowed Marc and me to focus on Brooke. I can never thank you enough."

"You're welcome. I wanted to help. I love those babies. I… I miss them."

Anne looked thoughtful as she nodded. "We'd love to have you come back, but I know it's probably not what you want to do."

"I want to." She hadn't been expecting this. Her heart softened.

"Really? After Marc… Well, I don't know exactly what happened, but I can guess." She stared at the throw pillow again for a beat. "Marc takes his responsibilities very seriously. He had to grow up awfully quick. It's made me happy—hopeful—to see how he is with you. I like that you bring out his softer side. But it was wrong of him to expect you to not open your business in the corner building. It's yours, Reagan. And Brooke and I will be the first in line on opening day. We want you to succeed."

Relief and gratitude chased away her anxiety. "I didn't expect to hear that."

"I wish I'd been able to get to know you better these weeks, because then you'd know I think the world of you. We can never repay you for all your help, but we will always appreciate it."

What a kind woman. "There's nothing to repay. I know how important it is for family to stick together when trouble hits. You and Marc and Brooke needed each other, and I was happy to be there for the babies. Plus, I had time on my hands. God worked it all out."

"He did." Anne nodded. "Look, my son means well when it comes to my bakery—I take the blame since I talked about nothing else for years—but he should never have expected you to change your plans. Like I said, he takes his responsibilities seriously, and in his mind, that includes Brooke and me. I'm trying to set him straight."

"Yeah, well…" It was the opening she needed. "I actually have something I want to discuss with you, and it has nothing to do with Marc."

"What's that?"

"This is going to sound out there, so you're just going to have to take my word for it that this is truly what I want."

"Okay."

"When Marc and I opened the bakery that Sunday your employee couldn't come in, I immediately pictured my chocolate shop there. The entire vision for it came to me. I'm talking every detail. From tearing down walls, reconfiguring the displays, replacing the floors, to changing the color of the paint. All of it."

"My bakery?" Anne's eyes grew round. "That tiny slice of square footage?"

"Yes."

"But Marc said your permit went through."

"It did." She opened her hands and shrugged. "I don't think it's right for me. It's too big. All I really need is enough space to make the chocolates. The actual front reception area can be small. I have no plans to add seating, and most of the kitchen will be converted to an open workspace."

Anne blinked. "What exactly are you saying?"

"What if we swapped?" Reagan's voice grew stronger as she spoke. This felt right. More than right. "I don't know if you own your building or lease it, but I'd like to open my chocolate shop there. And you can open your bakery in my building."

Tears formed in Anne's eyes as she shook her head in wonder. "I couldn't take it from you. It's *your* dream, Reagan. I can't help thinking Marc is behind this."

She really was a lovely woman. Reagan liked her more and more.

"No." She smiled widely. "He actually doesn't know about it. I couldn't discuss my plans with him, and I kept trying to ignore how much your bakery would fit my needs. Like I said, this doesn't change anything between me and your son. I'm sorry. He's just not the right man for me."

Anne's face fell, but she nodded. "I understand. And I don't blame you. I love him, and I would love nothing more than for the two of you to be together, but…he needs to get his priorities straight. He needs to value you."

Why did his own mother understand and he didn't?

"Do you own the bakery?" Reagan asked.

"I do. I leased it the first three years, and then I bought it."

"Good. We'll have to figure out how to handle the legal aspects. Get them appraised. If you buy my building and I buy yours, I want a clause that I would get the first option to buy it back if you ever decided to sell in the future. It's a special building."

"Deal." Anne's eyes shimmered with hope. Reagan could see why his mom's happiness was so important to him. She was an easy person to love.

"What do you say we make an appointment with a real-estate lawyer early next week? Get this plan set in motion? And I'll talk to Ed McCaffrey about the logistics of renovating both buildings."

"I would love that." Anne stood and they embraced. "Thank you. For making my dream come true. I still can't believe it. If there's anything you ever need, I want to be the first person you call."

They chatted all the way to the front door. And when Reagan waved goodbye to her, her heart was full.

She'd made the right choice for herself and her business.

She just wished things could have worked out with Marc, too.

Chapter Fourteen

Marc was nothing like his father. He drove through town Wednesday afternoon with his heart beating double-time. A large bouquet of red roses was on the passenger seat.

The horseback ride around the ranch earlier had given him clarity. He loved every inch of his land, and he'd never let it go. Just like he loved his mom and sister and nieces—nothing could make him turn his back on them.

His father had turned his back on all of them, taken what he wanted and vanished. But Marc wasn't like that. And Mom was right, too. God's faithfulness had kept them together—had kept *him* together all these years. And that had led him to the uncomfortable truth—he loved Reagan, and nothing could make him leave her. Not even the guilt over his mistakes.

Marc slowed his truck for the stop sign up ahead.

Sure, he'd messed up. He'd probably nuked any chance that Reagan would ever trust him again. But the fresh air and the stillness of the ride had reminded him he wasn't the sum of his mistakes. He'd prayed about it. Asked for forgiveness for not trusting God enough.

God *had* provided for them all these years. And God had graciously spared Brooke from death or permanent disability. He'd also sent Reagan to them precisely when they'd needed her the most.

When Marc needed her the most.

Why hadn't he seen it? Why hadn't he recognized how wrong it was to insist she put her dreams on the back burner for his mom's?

No matter how things played out, he had to apologize to Reagan. He needed her to know in no uncertain terms how much she meant to him. How much he regretted not supporting her plans.

In a few short minutes, he'd be at Reagan's door, and he could only pray she would let him in.

What if she didn't? He'd find a way to make her listen. Throw pebbles at her window. Sing outside her door. Anything. He'd do anything to get her to hear his apology.

He slowed to turn down her street. His nerves grew tighter as the first block went by. He was almost to her house when he saw his mother get into her car, back out of Reagan's driveway and head east.

What was his mom doing there?

Marc hoped she hadn't gone to ask Reagan to reconsider her plans for the building. If she had? He'd tell Reagan not to do it. Mom could keep the bakery where it was and find another building to expand in at some point. Reagan had poured too much into this to cave to his and his mother's demands.

He pulled into the driveway and grabbed the flowers. Before getting out, he smoothed his hand down his hair, adjusted his button-down shirt and took a deep breath. *God, You've come through for me over and over again. I don't deserve Reagan's love, but I don't deserve Yours, either. If she slams the door in my face or decides I'm not worth her time, help me remember I'm Yours and that's all that truly matters.*

Reagan's love mattered, too, though, and he couldn't pretend he wouldn't be devastated if she rejected him.

With long strides, he reached her door. Knocked twice. And waited.

What if his mom *had* tried to make Reagan change her mind? It didn't make sense, but why else would she be here? Dread pooled in his gut. He'd already given Reagan enough reasons to never talk to him again.

The door opened, and Reagan stood there looking like his every dream come true.

"What was my mom doing here? Did she try to talk you out of opening your chocolate shop? I didn't put her up to it. I wouldn't do that to you. I know you have no reason to believe me but—"

"Why don't you come inside?" The corner of her mouth curved up and her eyes twinkled. She didn't look mad. Didn't seem upset.

He followed her inside and shoved the flowers into her hand. *Real smooth.*

She held the blooms to her nose and closed her eyes as she inhaled their scent. "Let me get these into water."

"It can wait." He reached for her hand, but he wasn't quick enough. She'd already turned toward the kitchen.

"It will only take a sec."

"Reagan, what I have to say can't wait." He hurried after her—this time he did clasp her hand—and closed the distance between them. Took the flowers from her and set them on the counter. "I was wrong."

She dragged her gaze from the flowers to give him her full attention. "I know you were wrong."

Nothing if not direct. That was his Reagan.

"I never should have expected you to sacrifice your dream for my mother's. It was wrong and selfish and you didn't deserve that." He paused to take a deep breath. He was in over his head, but all he could do at this point was continue. "Regardless of what my mom told you just now, she and I had a long talk on Monday, and she told me she'd be okay without your building. And she will. So don't let her sway you. God will take care of her."

"You really believe that?" The words came out as wispy as a cloud.

"Yes." He nodded.

She tilted her head, her eyes searching his.

"I think God sent you here at a pivotal moment in my life," Marc said, "and I was too overwhelmed to see it. I knew you were an answer to a prayer my mom, my sister and I didn't even have time to pray. The twins needed you. We all needed you. But I needed you the most. I need you now. And tomorrow. And every day."

"What are you saying?"

"I love you, Reagan. I don't expect you to believe me after how I treated you, but I do. I love your generous heart. Mine is so small compared to yours. You remember the day Brooke had the stroke? I came home to the ranch and it was late. You were in the living room telling the twins a story. Not reading them one. Telling them one you made up. After hours and hours of taking care of infant babies you'd just met. I knew you were special even then."

Reagan was silent. Her eyes weren't twinkling. They were glistening with tears. He'd better get the rest out before she showed him the door.

"I'm sorry, Reagan. I'm sorry for being such an idiot. My priorities have shifted. Believe it or not, Mom helped me get them in line."

"I believe it." The tiniest of smiles appeared on her lips.

"Before you came along, I refused to make room in my life or in my heart for a woman. I already had four relying on me, or so I thought. But you wiggled in there and, instead of being a burden, you were a blessing, a comfort. I could listen to you explain how to make all the chocolates for hours. I could watch you kissing Alice's and Megan's cheeks and singing them silly songs every day for the rest of my life. I could talk about anything your heart desires as we share a pizza on your couch—and I want to. I want to share it all with you, Reagan. You told me you would never be as important to me as my mom, my sister and the twins. But you were wrong. You already are more important—I was just too stubborn to see it."

* * *

Reagan's heart was bursting with love, but she had to be certain she could trust him. Had to verify he truly was capable of putting her first.

"If I told you your mom asked me to give her the store and I did, what would you say?" She held her breath, hoping for the right words but bracing herself for the wrong ones. What if he simply thanked her? Hugged her and told her she'd just made his mom the happiest woman alive? She'd have to politely ask him to leave. Because that wasn't putting her first.

"Did she?" His face looked stricken. Then the muscle in his cheek pulsed. "Don't worry. I'll talk to her. You are *not* giving her your store. You've worked too hard to get to this point. I know I was a jerk about you inheriting it. I acted like you didn't deserve it—I'm sorry for treating you that way. I'm ashamed for thinking it in the first place. You *do* deserve it, Reagan, and I want to help you with it. Whatever you need, I'll be there, whether it's help painting or making sure the work is getting done. You can count on me."

"Your mom didn't ask me for the store." Her insides lit up like a carnival ride. Marc really *did* love her. "You should know your mom better than that. She stopped by to thank me for all my help."

He ran his fingers through his hair and sighed. "You're right. I don't know what's wrong with me."

"It's okay." She put her hand on his arm. "You've been through a lot this month."

"You've gotten me through a lot this month." He moved closer. "I don't know what I'd do without you, Reagan. I don't want what we have to end."

"I don't, either." She averted her eyes. "I have something to tell you."

His face went blank. "What is it?"

"Ever since I helped you that Sunday at the bakery, I've been having doubts about opening my shop in the corner building."

"But it's perfect for you. It has all that character and the big picture windows."

"It does have character, and I do love those windows." She nodded. "But it took all of two minutes in your mom's bakery for me to picture having my shop there."

"No." He shook his head. "You're just saying that to make me happy. I won't let you give up your dream."

Those words melted her even more than all his previous ones.

"Marc, listen to me. I could picture it—all of it—I could see every detail. And it feels right."

"Why didn't you say anything?"

"Because I was second-guessing myself."

"And I was pressuring you, which didn't help."

"It didn't."

"I'm sorry." He leaned down and touched his forehead to hers. "I'm really sorry."

She wrapped her arms around his back and hugged him. He held her tightly. After a few moments, she looked up at him.

"Your mom and I are swapping buildings. I don't know exactly how it will work, but we're setting up a meeting with a lawyer. We're both going to have our dreams come true, Marc, and I'm not doing it for you. I'm doing it for me. It's important you know that."

He frowned a moment. Then his face cleared and he nodded. "Yes. I understand. You're strong. Made of steel and surrounded by whimsy. You broke the mold, Reagan Mayer."

Steel and whimsy? She laughed. Yeah, she'd take it. It might be the best compliment anyone ever gave her.

"I fell in love with you, too, Marc." It felt so good to say the words out loud. "Your greatest gift—your loyalty—is all I wanted. And I hope you know it is a blessing. The fact you'd sacrifice anything for your loved ones makes you oh so appealing to me. I love how much you care. About the cattle and the ranch. About this town.

And most of all, about those sweet little babies and your mom and sister."

"Say it again." He smoothed her hair away from her face, looking deep into her eyes.

"I love you, Marc."

His lips were on hers—at first a whisper-like touch, then firmer, but tentative, as if asking if it was possible that she loved him. She kissed him back. Yes, she loved him.

She'd finally found the man she'd been longing for. The elusive man who got her. The one she could count on. A man who respected her. Her hot cowboy. Imagine that.

Chapter Fifteen

He had a full day planned, and this was the first stop. Marc held Reagan's hand the next morning as they walked into his living room. Brooke was sitting on the couch with Megan, and Gracie was putting Alice in her bouncy seat.

"Good morning, Gracie. I'd like you to meet Reagan Mayer. Reagan, Gracie French."

"It's nice to meet you." Gracie glanced up with a smile. Gracie and Brooke had been friends forever. With long blond hair, a curvy figure and a smile for everyone, Gracie hadn't changed much since Marc had last seen her before she'd moved to Idaho.

"You, too."

Marc kept a firm grip on Reagan's hand and continued forward until they reached Brooke. "We have something to tell you. You were sleeping last night or I would have told you then."

"Ok-a-ay." Brooke's dark blue eyes couldn't have grown bigger.

"Reagan and I are dating. It's new, but it's serious. I love her." He turned to Reagan and grinned, wanting to kiss her again, but he'd already kissed her a minute ago as he'd helped her out of his truck in the driveway.

"That's the best news." Keeping a firm grip on Megan, Brooke struggled to her feet. He wanted to take the baby, but he also knew how important it was for her to continue everyday tasks on her own. Once standing, she hugged Reagan and let her take the baby before turning to hug him. "I'm thrilled for you both."

"Really?" he asked.

"Of course." She beamed and wiped away the moisture from her eyes. Then she turned to Reagan. "You couldn't do better than my big brother. I'm so happy you two are together."

"I am, too." Reagan caressed the back of Megan's head. "I missed you this week. Look at you—you got up so quickly with the baby this time."

"I know. Isn't it great?" Brooke said. "I still need help, though. Are you up for coming back next week? Just in the mornings?"

"Yes! I've missed the babies so much."

"I hope you know you are always welcome

here." Brooke put her hands on Reagan's shoulders. "Always."

They shared a long look before Brooke stepped back. "I've been enjoying this week with Gracie."

"It's nice of you to help," Reagan said to Gracie. As the women chatted, Marc grew antsy.

"Listen, we've got to go." He kissed Brooke on the cheek.

"Already?"

"Yeah. We're stopping by Winston Ranch to see Erica, and then we have plans."

"A date." Reagan grinned.

"Well, don't let us keep you." Brooke took the baby from her.

Marc kissed Megan's cheek, then went over to Alice and tickled under her chin. Reagan, too, said goodbye to the babies. He reached for her hand and led her back outside.

Last night, they'd told his mom they were dating, and she'd actually burst into tears and hugged Reagan again and again, saying she'd made all of her dreams come true and that the Lord worked in mysterious ways.

In the driveway, he opened the passenger door to his truck and lifted Reagan by the waist to help her into the seat. Her laugh filled the air. "I could have gotten in by myself."

"Yeah, but I wanted to help. I can't get enough

of you." He leaned in and kissed her, loving it when she wrapped her arms around his neck and kissed him back.

"Oh, my." She touched her lips.

She could say that again. He grinned, shut her door and loped around to the driver's side. Soon they were driving past his pastures and onto the main road.

"Tell me again about the peppermint thing you're working on." He glanced her way. She exuded contentment, and there were those twinkles in her eyes as she faced him.

"I found the richest dark chocolate to enhance the peppermint filling. It's going to be amazing when I get the proportions right. I'm using a mold for them, but I think I need to order a different shape…"

And just like that, he was in her world. A world of candy delights and possibilities.

A world he hadn't known he needed and couldn't imagine living without.

"I have so much to tell you." Reagan and Marc were sitting on stools at the island in Erica's kitchen. Reagan had already hugged Rowan when they'd walked in, and she'd gone to his room to check out his new toy tractor. Then Gemma had bundled him up to get to know his "horsey" with Dalton. Two small horses had arrived last week for Dalton to teach his son, Grady, and Rowan how to ride this summer.

"Obviously." Erica gave Marc a pointed glance that said she didn't quite trust him. "You two want coffee?"

"Yes," they said in unison.

She laughed. "Okay, then." She pulled out three mugs from the cupboard and filled them all. Then she set one in front of Reagan, one in front of Marc, and after she poured cream in her own, she slid the carton their way.

"We had a long talk yesterday." Reagan glanced at him and took his hand.

"I messed up." Marc stared at Erica. "I was wrong. I treated your sister badly, and I regret it. I apologized."

Erica narrowed her eyes, sipped her coffee and said, "Good."

"But before Marc came over, I made a decision. You might not understand it." It was important for Reagan to get this right. She didn't want her sister or the rest of her family to have any doubts where her intentions were concerned. "For a while now, I've been having a lot of second thoughts about using the corner building for my shop."

Erica frowned.

"But there is one spot in town…well, as soon as I saw it, I could picture my shop there. I know it's crazy. I know you're not going to understand. But I want to open R. Mayer Chocolates in Annie's Bakery. We're swapping buildings."

Reagan held her breath, bracing herself for the judgment sure to come.

Erica seemed to consider it, then lifted her chin. "You know, Reagan, I'm not surprised."

"You're not?" Her stomach clenched as she waited for her to say she was making a mistake.

"No." Erica placed her mug on the counter. "Tell me the truth, though. Are you doing this for you? Or for him?" She jerked her thumb to Marc. Reagan glanced his way, but he didn't seem offended.

"For me." As she thought about the new smaller shop, she couldn't stop a smile from spreading across her face. "I don't know why, but something just felt off about the corner building. And I talked to Blaine yesterday, and it just clicked. I guess I feel a bit like Goldilocks. My building was too big."

"And Annie's Bakery isn't too small?" Erica asked.

"No. It's just right."

Her sister hitched her chin to Marc. "What do you think about all this? You got what you wanted."

He squeezed Reagan's hand. The look he gave her was full of love.

"I did get what I want—your sister. I love her. Whatever makes her happy makes me happy."

Erica softened at that. "And if she changed her mind? Decided to open her shop in the corner building after all?"

"I'd help with anything she needed. I want *all* her dreams to come true."

That was why she loved him. Reagan let out a heartfelt sigh. "Thank you."

"Well said." Erica pointed to him. "Okay, Marc. Why don't you check out the new horse with Dalton while I talk to my sister?"

He glanced at Reagan and she nodded. She needed to make sure Erica truly understood where she was coming from. Marc rose from the stool and kissed her temple. "Is it all right if I take the coffee with me?"

"It's all yours."

A few minutes later, Reagan tried to mentally unravel the knots in her stomach as she prepared for a lecture from Erica.

"Do you trust him?" Erica asked. She looked more vulnerable than Reagan had ever seen.

"I do. He's sincere. I made the decision to swap buildings with his mom for my own sake, not for his."

Erica nodded, a thoughtful expression in her eyes. "Do you love him?"

"Yes."

"You know, I would have understood if you'd decided to let his mom have your building for his sake."

"You would have?" Reagan was surprised. Her sister always had such vocal opinions about her life.

"Yeah, I would have. But, man, I'm proud of you, Reag. That took guts. To know what you really wanted. When you told Anne to take the building, you weren't going to take Marc back, were you?"

"No, I wasn't." She shook her head as a sense of pride expanded in her chest. All her life she'd wanted her family to be proud of her. But most of all, she wanted to be proud of herself. And she was.

"Now I know you two are meant to be. He loves you. It's written all over his face, and I don't think you'll ever have to worry again about not being his top priority."

"I hope not."

Erica rounded the counter and pulled her into a hug. Reagan sank into her embrace.

"I'm glad I moved here," she said as they separated.

"I'm glad you did, too." She raised her mug. "To Great-Uncle Dewey and Great-Aunt Martha. If it wasn't for them, we wouldn't be here."

"We found our purpose—"

"And our partners—"

"Right here in Jewel River."

They clinked mugs.

"Now, let's go see what those guys are up to." Erica waggled her eyebrows and Reagan laughed. They linked arms as they headed out into the sunshine, giggling all the way to the paddock where Dalton had Rowan on his hip and Marc was petting the forehead of the new horse.

"We all good?" Marc asked Erica.

She grinned, let go of Reagan's arm and went over to give him a hug. "We're all good."

"Phew." He pretended to wipe his forehead. Then he reached for Reagan's hand. "And how are you? Ready for phase two of our day?"

She leaned into his side. "I'm ready."

"Then what are we waiting for?"

This. This was what she'd been waiting for. Her entire life. The man who got her, and the one she couldn't wait to spend her days with. "Let's go."

Epilogue

After fifteen years of patiently waiting, his mother's dream of expanding her bakery was about to come true. Tomorrow was the grand opening.

All because of the beautiful woman by his side. Marc held out a chair for Reagan at the Jewel River Legacy Club meeting. It had been four months since they'd declared their love for each other, and he couldn't believe how much had happened in that time.

Once his mom and Reagan had hammered out the details of selling each other their buildings, Ed McCaffrey and his crew had undertaken the renovations of both locations. His mother had decided to temporarily close the bakery to give her more time with Brooke and the twins until the renovations were complete. Marc had never seen her happier.

Brooke had healed from the stroke with only a slight limp remaining. Marc wished he could take away her fear of having another stroke, but the doctors had warned her she was at a higher risk. All he could do was leave it in God's hands. Mom had moved back to town, and since it was a one-story house and easy to walk to everything, Brooke and the girls had moved in with her. They were all doing well.

Meanwhile, Reagan's vision for her chocolate shop had come true, from opening up the kitchen down to the floating shelves she'd pictured all those months ago. She'd spent these months honing her recipes and finalizing every aspect of the products, from the wrappers the chocolates sat in to the special packaging system she'd worked out. R. Mayer Chocolates would start taking online orders early next week.

"Did Alice start crawling yet?" Reagan leaned in with a whisper to Marc as Erica readied her notes at the head of the table.

"Not yet. She's on all fours, shifting back and forth. It's only a matter of time."

"I was sure she'd take off yesterday." She shook her head. At least three days a week, Reagan went over to Mom's house to spend time with Brooke and the twins. "Megan won't be far behind."

"Thank you for coming, everyone." Erica's

voice carried. "It's great to be back in the new—and improved—community center."

"It doesn't smell anymore." Christy Moulten looked around in wonder and turned to her son, sitting next to her. "Cade, I still think you should use the Winston for your wedding reception. Erica, yours was lovely. Truly impressive."

Reagan raised her eyebrows and glanced at Marc. "Is Cade dating anyone?"

"Not that I know of." He shrugged.

"Is there something you aren't telling me, Mom?" Cade asked dryly. "Don't tell me you ordered a bride through the internet for me."

"Smarty-pants." She made a *tsk tsk* sound and playfully slapped his arm. "If I could order both of you boys brides, I would."

"They don't want to get married," Clem said loudly in his exasperated tone. "Worry about yourself, woman."

"Me? I have just about had it with you, Clem." Flames could have shot out from Christy's gaze and Marc wouldn't have been surprised.

Cade motioned for Erica to keep going.

Everyone stood to say the Pledge of Allegiance and the Lord's Prayer. Then Erica smiled at the people seated around the tables. "First, I want to thank Angela Zane and her grandson, Joey, for their exciting film. I have to admit, watching *Romeo & Juliet: Wyoming Style* on the makeshift screen in the park last month was a lot of fun."

"The whole town turned out for it." Angela's bright eyes glowed as she nodded. "When we could only get three actors on board, I thought Shakespeare-in-the-Park was done for. But my Joey knew better. He said, 'Nana, it doesn't have to be live. I'll film it, and those three can play all the parts.' We're so proud of him."

"I don't recall the book having Juliet fall from a hayloft into a pile of cow patties after Romeo tells her he loves her," Clem said. "Ditto for the bull charging at her."

"Wasn't that scene with the bull electrifying?" Angela seemed to not notice Clem's sarcasm.

Erica turned to Mary Corning. "Thank you for setting up the crew for the kettle corn. It really added to the overall experience."

Mary smiled smugly. "I'm telling you we should install the equipment in the park for anyone to use. Who doesn't love kettle corn?"

"Yes, well, we've been over this before. Remember? The safety issues?" Erica gave her an apologetic smile. "Now, let's move on to the next order of business."

"Erica?" Cade stood. "I have an update."

"Go ahead."

"The veterinarian will be moving to town in

the spring. She and her father have finally gotten their plans in order."

"Good job. Thank you for taking the lead on this. Anyone else?" Erica glanced around until her gaze landed on Marc. He nodded and stood.

"First, Reagan and I have an announcement. I proposed this weekend, and she agreed to be my wife."

A round of congratulations and applause filled the room. When it calmed down, Marc continued. "Tomorrow is the grand reopening of Annie's Bakery. I hope you all will go over to the new building and show your support. She sure is excited." Then he looked at Reagan and his heart filled with love. "And Reagan's chocolates will be for sale online beginning next week."

"When are you going to open the store for us to buy them?" Clem asked.

"Hopefully, soon. But feel free to stop in anytime, Clem. I'm making some new caramels for you."

"I'm taking you up on that, girly." He pointed to her and winked.

Johnny Abbot raised his hand.

"Yes, Johnny?"

"I just wanted to say how nice it is to see you all working together. Since I started coming to these meetings, you've gotten a new welcome sign for the town made up, added the nicest flowers along Center Street, gotten the whole town together for the Shakespeare film Angela's grandson made, and now we have two freshly renovated buildings downtown. This club has already made a lot of progress. I can't wait to see what you all will come up with next."

Marc took Reagan's hand under the table and squeezed it. "He's right, you know."

"I know." She smiled at him. "Jewel River is my favorite place to be."

"Wherever you are is my favorite place to be."

* * * * *

If you enjoyed this Wyoming Legacies story, be sure to pick up the previous book in Jill Kemerer's miniseries:

The Cowboy's Christmas Compromise

Available now from Love Inspired!

Dear Reader,

Sometimes our path seems obvious and straight, and then complications arise that make us wonder if we're on the right path after all. Reagan was sure of her plan to open the chocolate shop in the corner building, and Marc was certain his future only included the ranch, his mom, his sister and the twins. But with Brooke's stroke came a series of events that had them questioning their future and themselves.

Life isn't always easy. Just because the path gets hard to follow and we can't see exactly where it ends doesn't mean we're on the wrong one. We can trust God through the ups and downs and twists and turns. He'll always be with us. He'll always love us. Just keep praying for Him to guide you when the going is rough.

I hope you enjoyed this book in the Wyoming Legacies series. I love connecting with readers. Feel free to email me at jill@jillkemerer. com or write me at PO Box 2802, Whitehouse, Ohio, 43571.

Blessings to you,
Jill Kemerer